FIGHTING FOR HAILEY

Redemption Harbor® Security

Katie Reus

ABOUT THE BOOK

She's the one who got away...

They grew up together, dated for years—but when Jesse Lennox had a chance at a college scholarship and a new life, Hailey abruptly ended things. She wanted him to have the life he deserved, and with her track record, she knew she'd just bring him down. Now they're both grown, and she runs the new division of Redemption Harbor Consulting, heading up their security branch. But her past is about to collide with her present in a big way, and she can't outrun her demons any longer.

This time, he's playing for keeps...

Years ago, Hailey joined the military and ruthlessly cut all her foster siblings out of her life. Now that one of them is in danger, she's back—and Jesse isn't letting her push him away ever again. One of their own has been kidnapped, and with the clock ticking, they have no choice but to work together to find him before it's too late. But the threat is much worse than they imagined. It will take all their combined skills—and breaking through Hailey's walls—to unravel the clues in time to save him.

CHAPTER 1

—Day drinking? Don't mind if I do.—

Hailey couldn't believe how lax Easton's security was as she broke in through a side window. Sure, the window was only accessible after she'd rappelled down from the roof of the six-story condo building, after temporarily blocking the building's security cameras. But still, he should have had *all* of his windows secured.

She'd kick his ass later for the oversight—once she figured out where the hell he was and who'd kidnapped him.

And once she knew he was alive. Because he just had to be. She refused to believe anything else.

Her sweet foster brother, whom she'd cut out of her life years ago, along with two other foster brothers. She couldn't think about that right now, couldn't think about any of them. Especially since Easton had reached out recently, wanted to catch up.

And she'd agreed to lunch since she'd been in town anyway on a job, and then at the last minute she'd canceled—because she was an asshole. Also because of her deep-seated abandonment issues and guilt at cutting him out so thoroughly years ago. She *knew* she had issues, would likely drown in them one day because of her own cowardice. And therapy sure as shit hadn't helped.

If she'd met up with Easton yesterday for lunch, he wouldn't have been kidnapped. And even though she knew that, sure, technically his kidnapping wasn't her fault, she was feeling the blame for ghosting him.

She wanted to scream at the world right now.

Hopefully, she could make up for it and find out who the hell had taken him—and save him. She owed him that much. And then she'd make his kidnappers pay. But that was for another day. She had to focus on the first step—finding something that could help her track Easton down.

If she had to guess why he'd been taken, it was because of something he'd been working on. The man was a gentle giant, a gifted scientist who only wanted to make the world a better place. He'd already made huge headway on research for ALS and was apparently working on something else that had the scientific community abuzz.

As she slid from the window opening into his living room, she quickly scanned the place, not surprised that it was shockingly neat. Even his gray and white throw pillows were fluffed up perfectly on each end of the bigger couch. He'd always been like that, with nothing out of place.

No television in his living room—no surprise—but bookshelves lined two of the walls. And they were filled with some she'd read and most she probably wouldn't understand. All science-related stuff way out of her wheelhouse, but she scanned them nonetheless, looking for anything out of place.

Her gaze snagged on an old photograph, and she froze, staring at four kids. They'd all been lined up: Easton, Cash, her, and Jesse. They'd all had their arms around each other, standing in that order. Jesse had been the bookend next to her, pulling her close. Possessively. And she'd been tucked up against Jesse as if that was exactly where she belonged.

Jesus, they'd been young. A handful of sixteen- and seventeen-year-olds who'd already seen the worst the world had to offer.

But that had been a really good year—the best of her life. The year before everything had gone to shit.

Shaking off the memory of that day, she snagged the small frame off the bookshelf, then tucked it into her backpack before she moved to the kitchen.

She'd come back to the bookshelves later, but first she wanted to look at a couple spots where she thought Easton might have hidden something. Because he'd always been like that, squirreling stuff away. Hell, they all had. They'd hidden personal shit they couldn't easily take with them, and old habits die hard.

Maybe she was wrong and nothing would come of her search today, but she had to try.

Because it had been ten hours since his kidnapping, and the cops were useless. She could move a lot faster than they could, and she didn't need to worry about pesky things like warrants and the law. Nothing would stop her from finding Easton.

If she could just figure out what the hell he'd been working on. Because this had to be related to his job since the man didn't appear to have a personal life.

She'd already started digging into Easton's financials, and so far they seemed normal enough, but she'd be doing a deep dive as well.

When her phone buzzed, she glanced at the caller ID and slid in her earpiece as she moved into the kitchen. "Hey."

"Hey yourself," Reese said, her tone light. "Done breaking into your friend's place?"

"In the process."

"Any issues?"

"Nah, I'm good."

"Okay. But I want to go on record as being annoyed that you didn't ask for backup. And that you didn't do this the easy way. You could have just called—"

"Is the only reason you called to bitch at me?"

"That would imply I'm being unreasonable, and I'm not. You should have brought backup. And you should have called your old foster brother! He'd have let you into Easton's condo."

"You're annoying when you're logical."

"Did you... Did you just agree with me?" Reese whispered.

Hailey rolled her eyes as she moved into the kitchen.

"Don't roll your eyes at me."

"Can you see me?" She glanced around the big space, looking for any electronics Reese might have hacked into, because Hailey wouldn't put it past the talented woman.

"No, I just know you. And I want to go on record again as saying you need to get over your trust issues. You'll never be able to move on and have a real life or relationship until you do that."

Hailey pulled in a steadying breath, praying to a god she wasn't sure existed for a bucketful of patience. Because holy shit, enough with the lectures. She knew she was screwed up and lonely; she certainly didn't need anyone to remind her of that.

"That said," Reese continued, "the real reason I called is to update you on the Urichko job."

"And you couldn't have texted?" Hailey pulled out the trash can under the kitchen sink, then moved the neatly organized cleaning supplies out of the way. He'd even put them in order by size and color. Man, she really missed Easton. She knocked on the bottom of the cabinet, trying to see if there was a false panel, but couldn't find any seams when she felt around.

"Well, yeah, but I wanted to remind you that I think what you're doing is dumb, and I love being right. *Also*, I thought you'd want to hear this directly from me. I found what I needed on that sorry excuse for a teacher."

"Oh yeah?" Belinda Urichko was a high school teacher who had no business teaching, so even though this was so far out of their realm of normal work, Hailey and Reese had taken the job for free.

Normally they took jobs for people who were desperate, who had no one to turn to, those who'd been bullied by the system that was supposed to protect them. This didn't exactly fall into that category, but it was still a worthy case.

After putting back everything in the kitchen, Hailey walked to the guest bathroom, moved everything out of the cabinet under the sink, and started feeling around—*bingo*.

"Yep. Complaints from her three previous schools. They weren't easily accessible, and it's clear they were intentionally buried. And there's a hidden relationship with the current director of her school."

"What kind of relationship?" Hailey managed to pry off the bottom of the cabinet to reveal a hollowed-out area with a laptop in a plastic bag. She pulled it out then quickly put everything back in place.

"Cousins through marriage, so I'm guessing that's how she got the job."

"Good work. I'll call you back when I'm done, get more details."

"Okay. Are you sure you're fine doing this alone? I don't like that you're without backup."

"Yeah, but thanks." Normally they worked in pairs for any recon, but this was different. No one had hired them. She was doing this to help a friend, and no one had any idea she was here. The threat level was minimal. "I'll be heading back to the rental soon."

They'd rented a place here a couple weeks ago for another job, then the Urichko one had landed in their lap, and then... Easton had been kidnapped.

If Hailey believed in kismet, she might think she was supposed to be in the Virginia area. And maybe she'd already screwed up because fate had given her the opportunity to have lunch with Easton and save him, and she'd blown it.

"I think I found something good," Hailey continued, burying thoughts of fate and all that bullshit. "But I'm going to do another sweep." She just wished she knew what she was looking for. The laptop might not even matter, but she was going to check it out anyway. Why keep it hidden if it wasn't important?

"See you soon." As Reese disconnected, there was an alert on the building's security cameras, reminding her that she needed to reset the system again on another loop so she'd have more time to search.

After doing just that, she moved to the bedrooms, pushing down the guilt at invading Easton's home. It was certainly nice, nothing like the places they'd bounced around in when they'd been kids. And clean too, which was no surprise. Big windows that let in a lot of natural light, and everything was in neutral shades—because anything too bright bothered Easton. At least if it overwhelmed a room or a space. As an adult, he'd clearly managed to create a space that mitigated his sensory issues, and she found tears pricking her eyes that he'd done so well for himself. That he'd created a wonderful space that was all his.

And whoever'd taken him had better pray for mercy.

Gritting her teeth, she stepped out of his bedroom into the hallway, planning to make her way to the guest room or office next, and found herself staring down the barrel of a gun.

She blinked, her eyes locking on the bluest eyes she'd ever seen. They belonged to a tall, lean god who deigned to walk among mere mortals.

Jesse Lennox.

Her first love, her first *everything*, the man she'd never gotten over—the one whose heart she'd had to break so he would move on from her.

She sucked in a breath as the world actually stood still. Time forgot how to move as she stared into those soulful eyes. And she knew that in a few hundred years all the calendars would be off by juuuust a fraction because of this very moment. When the only sunshine she'd ever had in her life walked right back into it.

CHAPTER 2

—It wasn't a fall, but a crash.—

"Hailey," Jesse breathed out even as he sheathed his pistol, tucked it neatly underneath his jacket. Nausea swelled in him that he'd pulled a weapon on her, even inadvertently.

Her tawny brown eyes widened as she stared up at him, clearly as shocked as he was. She still kept her dark hair long, and today it was pulled back in a simple braid. The rest of her clothing was nondescript—dark pants, dark sneakers, and a long-sleeved black shirt tucked into her pants. She was the hottest burglar to ever walk the earth, he imagined.

The fiery star who'd crashed into his life years ago, then left his heart in cinders when she'd walked out of it.

Words. Find some, he ordered himself.

She recovered first, hitching her backpack up slightly as she glared. "What the hell are you doing here?"

He wasn't sure why she was shouting. Or why the hell she was here. But he drank in the sight of her as he held up the key, his tone dry. "I have a key. And my fingerprints are programmed on the biometric lock. What are *you* doing here?"

And how the hell had she gotten in?

"The cops are incompetent and have no leads on Easton. I've started running his financials and thought I might find something law enforcement missed."

"You want to help find Easton?" After she'd abandoned all of them? He stared hard at her.

"Of course I do!" She was back to shouting and seemed offended he would ask.

"The Feds are involved too now." Because he'd called in favors and demanded they take over.

"Since when?"

"Since an hour ago—and they'll be stopping by here soon enough."

She cursed under her breath, then shot him a hard glare, those tawny brown eyes flinty. "Are you going to turn me in for breaking in?"

"I'm going to ignore that question." He glanced over his shoulder, looking down the hallway, still wondering how she'd gotten in. "How the hell did you break in here anyway?"

It was six floors up. He was here only because security had alerted him to some glitches in the camera feeds. As Jesse turned around, Hailey was already moving past him, making her way to the front of the condo—and not answering him. "Answer the question, Hailey."

She swiveled to face him, her expression carefully blank, and he hated it. "You want to know, fine. I hacked into the camera system, put the security feed on a loop, used the back entrance to the stairs to gain entrance to the roof, then basically rappelled down onto Easton's patio. Though rappelled is a bit of stretch. I basically dropped down on a rope. From there, I got in through one of his windows—which he needs to fix when he gets back. I would have broken into his front door but wasn't sure what kind of biometrics he had and didn't want to waste the time or risk running into any neighbors. For the record, *all* his windows should be secured."

And she seemed absolutely indignant that they weren't.

He blinked, realized she was dead serious. Well, that explained the camera glitches. "You could have just called me. Or Cash."

"Okay, yeah sure. I'm sure you guys would have loved to hear from me."

He ignored her response because it was asinine. "Did you find anything?" Because his only priority now was finding Easton—even if this blast from the past had knocked him on his ass. Maybe not literally, but holy hell, his brain was still catching up that the only woman he'd ever loved was standing in front of him, looking pissed off and even more gorgeous than before.

"No."

He narrowed his gaze because her nose did that little scrunch thing she'd always done when lying. It was subtle, but it was her tell. "Stop lying. What did you find? We can work together."

"I'm not working with the cops."

"I meant you and me." At a slight sound, he paused, frowned. Then he held a finger to his lips, and she nodded as he tugged her back down the hallway.

She ducked into the guest room and silently slid her backpack off as he pulled out his pistol again. He didn't normally carry, but after what had happened to Easton—one of his best friends being kidnapped in the middle of the day with no warning, no request for ransom, nothing—he was being extra careful. Both he and Cash were. They were worth a hell of a lot more than Easton, but it wasn't a secret they were all friends, and that Easton worked for Jesse. Which was why Jesse kept expecting a ransom, but so far nothing had come in.

The lack of ransom demand had him more worried than he wanted to admit to himself.

Moving quietly, Hailey withdrew a can of bear spray from her pack and pulled out the orange tab to unlock it. Then she slid on goggles that should have looked ridiculous but somehow looked adorable, because of course they did. He blinked in surprise at her weapon of choice, but turned back to the door as the faint sound of footsteps sounded from the kitchen area.

Stay here, he mouthed.

She lifted a dark eyebrow, which yep, that was about right. She'd never listened to anything, ever. Never believed she could be loved for just her.

Burying a sigh, he moved in front of her and eased out into the hallway. Before he'd taken a step, someone barreled into him, slamming him into the wall. His weapon clattered to the floor under the impact.

But he brought his elbow back, aiming for his attacker's temple. The only thing he could sense was that the guy was large and definitely male.

As he swiveled, the guy punched him in the side, clearly aiming for his kidney, but thankfully missing.

Jesse managed to keep his footing as he turned, then swept the masked man's legs out from under him in a sharp kick.

Cursing, the guy tumbled onto his back, but he was quick, struck out again with his feet.

Jesse dodged to the side when the man kicked out, clearly attempting to break his knee.

Before Jesse could move for his weapon, Hailey jumped in front of him and started spraying at the guy's face.

The man screamed, his balaclava doing nothing to stop the stream of capsaicin spewing over his eyes and into his nose.

"That's enough." Jesse wrapped his arm around her middle and tugged her back when she kept spraying, careful to stay behind her as the guy writhed on the hallway floor in agony.

Groaning, the man ripped his mask off as he tried to stand, but his eyes were swollen and he stumbled, bowled headfirst into the wall, and fell back on his ass with another cry of pain.

"Don't move, or I'll let her blast you again." Jesse kept his voice calm but hard as he plucked up his fallen weapon, held it on the red-eyed, snot-faced man, who was still cursing at them. "Find something to restrain him," he said to Hailey, not taking his eyes off the man on the floor.

Jesse kept enough distance that the man couldn't attack him from his position. Not that he was worried about the moaning guy. Jesse had training, and this man was a pathetic mess of snot and tears.

A few moments later Hailey returned, a thick cord in her hand, her goggles removed. When she went to move past him, he handed her his weapon. "Shoot him if necessary."

"Gladly." Her icy tone didn't surprise him.

The guy was still groaning but didn't fight him. Jesse rolled him over and secured his wrists behind his back, then tied up his ankles, careful not to get pepper spray on himself. Yeah, this guy wasn't going anywhere. Jesse patted him down, found no ID and no weapons.

"Can I get some water for my eyes? Or milk?" the guy called out as Jesse stepped away from him.

They both ignored him as they moved into the living room, as if they both had the same idea. Jesse kept the guy in his line of sight as he turned to Hailey. "You know him?"

She shook her head. "No. This has to be related to Easton being taken. Right?"

Hell if he knew. "It would stand to reason, yes. But we've got to call the Feds."

She gritted her teeth. "We should *question* him instead."

"That sounds a lot like *torture*."

Hailey simply shrugged, not looking apologetic, her tawny eyes hard. If Jesse was being honest, he didn't mind the thought of torturing someone related to kidnapping Easton either. But clearly he had to be the voice of reason.

"I'll call the Feds," he murmured as he pulled out his phone. If this was related to Easton's kidnapping, the FBI had just taken over and would need to question the guy.

"Great." Hailey stalked away from him and disappeared into the guest room. When she came back out, she had her backpack on and a small device in her hands.

"Don't—" He started to tell her not to approach the guy but stopped when Special Agent Robert Parker, the man in charge of the investigation, answered the phone. Jesse cleared his throat. "I'm at Easton's condo, and a man just broke in. He's secured, but I suggest you send someone down here to pick him up."

Jesse hung up without waiting for a response. Yes, it was a dick thing to do, but he didn't give a shit. He was just a civilian who'd done his duty by calling it in.

Ignoring his phone when it rang, he moved closer to the two of them as... Hailey took the man's fingerprints. *Okay, then.*

"I'm just grabbing his prints before the Feds get here," she murmured. Then louder as she stared down at the injured man, she said, "If you tell me why you're here, I'll wash your face off."

"Bite me," the man snarled, tears still streaming down his face. His eyes were bloodshot and he looked like a raccoon. Only instead of a black mask, his eyes were red-rimmed.

She made a sound of disgust. "Fine, have it your way."

The guy shifted his entire body, trying to knock her down even with his bound ankles, but she moved *fast*.

Hailey jumped up, her petite form easily missing the man's jerky attempt to swipe her feet out from under her. As she moved away from the guy, she tucked her little machine into her backpack and faced Jesse. "So, I'm going to go ahead and get out of here."

A bark of laughter escaped, but there was no humor in it as Jesse blocked her way. "You're not going anywhere."

CHAPTER 3

—*Whatever it takes.*—

"Yes, that's correct. Ms. West and I arrived together and were here for a few minutes alone, when he," Jesse nodded at the man being hauled out in cuffs, "broke in and attacked us."

Sure, it was a crime to lie to a Fed, but Jesse sure as shit wasn't going to tell them that Hailey had broken in. The only thing he cared about was finding his kidnapped friend, and he'd break all sorts of laws to do it.

If it came down to it, he'd simply say he gave her permission to enter via a rope and the outside patio. Because there was no planet in which he turned her over to the Feds or cops—for anything.

The man in cuffs snorted at Jesse, as if to call him a liar, but Jesse ignored him. And he also made note of the man's reaction, but tucked that away for later. Whoever he was, he shouldn't have known if they'd arrived separately unless he'd seen her break in—or seen Jesse arrive alone. Either way, it seemed possible that someone was watching this place.

Hailey ignored the guy too. If anything, she was ignoring *everyone*. She'd been unusually quiet as she sat on the couch next to him, her arms wrapped protectively around her backpack as Special Agent Parker questioned them.

And Jesse was feeling unusually protective of her. Or maybe it wasn't unusual. He hadn't seen her in nine years, two weeks, three days. But who was counting? Didn't mean his protectiveness over her had ever waned.

"We've answered your questions more than once." Hailey finally spoke again, meeting the agent in the eyes, that red-hot temper he remembered so well simmering just beneath the surface. Oh, that was never good. "Do we need a lawyer?"

"What? *No*." Agent Parker frowned as he looked between the two of them, clearly surprised by the question. "We're just trying to cover everything to understand what happened."

"Well you know what happened, and answering the same questions over and over won't do any good. And it sure won't help you find Easton. Where are you on that, by the way?" she demanded. "Because finding him is what matters right now."

He blinked, probably because while Hailey looked harmless and sweet, she was dynamite in a small package. A dark horse. "I can't talk about an ongoing investigation."

"Then I'm done here." She stood, slid her backpack on, and shot Jesse a challenging look.

"We're both done here. And since we arrived together, we'll be leaving together." He dared her to correct him, his own look just as challenging.

She gave him a smile that was ridiculously sweet—and fake to anyone who knew her well. "Sounds good to me."

Jesse turned back to the agent, who was watching them curiously. "The condo locks automatically when you leave, so unless you need us for anything..."

Sighing, the agent stood with them. "No. But I don't like this break-in. There's a chance this doesn't have anything to do with Easton Reed's kidnapping at all, but you." His tone was as pointed as his expression as he looked at Jesse.

"Why might this be about you?" He could hear the frown in Hailey's voice without looking at her.

Instead of answering her, Jesse shook the agent's hand, then wrapped his arm around Hailey to lead her out with him.

She jolted slightly, but didn't pull away until they got to the elevator. Then she nudged him back and put a foot of distance between them. Her posture was stiff, and it was clear she was avoiding his gaze as they stepped into the elevator.

"Where are you parked?" he asked.

"Nearby." She shoved her hands in her pockets and looked straight ahead as they descended, her jaw firmly set.

As if he was going to let her ignore him. "I'll drive you to your vehicle."

"No, thanks."

"I wasn't asking—and we're talking." But not in this elevator which was monitored and recorded. He'd wait until they were in his vehicle. "This way," he said when she started for the front of the lobby.

Sighing, she turned to look at him. "Look, Jesse, I appreciate you not narcing me out, but—"

He moved quickly, crowding against her before he reached behind her and unzipped her backpack. Then he pulled out the laptop inside. *Bingo*. He knew she'd had something in it; she'd been cradling it like it was her "precious."

Trapped against him as he rezipped the backpack, she nudged him once in the stomach. "What the hell are you doing, you freak?"

"This looks a lot like Easton's," he said, tucking it under one arm. There were a couple stickers on the front from a YouTube creator he liked. "I *knew* you found something in there." Keeping his voice low, Jesse glanced over as a Fed in a blue jacket strode through the lobby door, nodded politely at the guy. "So if you want to look at it, you're coming with me," he whispered.

"You are so..." She let out a little growling sound that was adorable, then shoved her hands back in her pockets, her expression calculating. "Fine, whatever. Let's go."

He'd missed her, had so many things he wanted to say, to *ask* her. Because now that he was older and had some distance, he'd started to realize why she'd ended things so abruptly with him. Or at least he thought he did. Maybe she really had just been done with him, as she'd told him before she'd literally left one morning and never looked back. Never responded to any of their calls, emails, or even letters when she'd been overseas.

"So what do you know about Easton's kidnapping?" Because if she was looking into it, she'd know more than what was on the news. Or he guessed.

She'd always been good with computers. She'd joined the Marines after high school, and from what he'd heard—aka researched personally—she'd been in Intel. Which made sense since she now ran a security branch of Redemption Harbor Consulting, Redemption Harbor Security.

She glanced around as they entered the parking garage, waited until she slid into the passenger seat of his Land Rover to finally talk. "I know that he was taken by pros. I got a copy of that doorbell recording. The two men who took him had on high-quality masks designed to block facial recognition software, but I don't think they ever planned to be seen on camera. That doorbell was a fluke, I'm guessing, given the angle and the fact that he managed to run from them temporarily." She closed her eyes and leaned her head back against the headrest. "I hate the thought of anything happening to Easton," she finally murmured.

"Me too." He started his vehicle and steered out of the parking lot, mainly so he wouldn't sit and stare at Hailey. Drink in every gorgeous inch of her.

It didn't matter that years had passed between them, she still got his heart racing without even trying. Just being near her had always done that. Ever since they were fifteen and got placed in a foster home that was basically a last hope for "problem kids." Whatever the hell that meant.

The day he'd met her, she'd knocked a kid out for picking on Easton for being gay—then she'd turned to Jesse and asked if he wanted some, her fists raised in defiance as she readied to take on someone twice her size. And *that* was the moment he'd fallen for her, fast and hard. No turning back after that.

"I hacked into some of the nearby CCTVs, but whoever took him was careful," she said. "I think they switched vehicles because I never picked up that van on any cameras except for once afterward. Then it's like it disappeared into thin air."

"You're right. They had to have switched. The Feds just found the van a couple hours ago, abandoned on the top floor of a parking garage. Where are you parked anyway?" Not that he planned to take her to her vehicle, but he could have someone pick it up and bring it to his place—because that was where he was taking her. He wasn't letting her out of his sight.

"Oh, I actually took an Uber and had it drop me off at a nearby coffee shop. Got a drink, then went for a 'stroll.' Figured I'd just call for one when I left Easton's."

He snorted softly. "I can't believe you nailed that asshole with bear spray."

She shrugged as she pulled out her phone. "You can just drop me off anywhere, and I'll grab a ride," she murmured, pulling up her list of favorited contacts.

He tried not to stare, hated that there was a list of names he didn't recognize. Because they weren't in each other's lives anymore. Hadn't been for a long time. Some days, he wondered if he'd ever known her at all or if those years together had been a fever dream.

"So are you ever going to explain why you abandoned all of us? Just cut ties as if we didn't live together for three years. As if you and I were strangers."

The words were out before he could stop himself, but if he was being brutally honest, he didn't *want* to stop himself. No amount of therapy was ever going to fix the giant Hailey-shaped hole inside him that she'd left. And he wanted answers.

Tawny brown eyes wide, she turned to stare at him as he pulled up to a red light. Yeah, he probably should have picked a better place than in the vehicle. Maybe he shouldn't have said anything at all. But for the first time in almost a decade, he had her under the same roof with him. He was going to say exactly what he wanted.

"You all did great without me around," was all she finally muttered as she tore her gaze away.

"So you're not answering. Never took you for a coward, Kitten." He used his old nickname for her, very much trying to get a rise out of her. Because sometimes that was the only way he'd been able to get her to respond to something she didn't want to talk about.

He'd take anything at this point as years of pain roiled to the surface and punched him right in his chest. He'd always told himself he'd be calm if he ever saw her again. Cool, calm, civilized. Apparently, he liked to lie to himself. He was never calm around her.

She sucked in a sharp breath. "Jesse." His name, one word. Nothing more.

And he felt that word all the way to his soul.

When it was clear she wasn't going to say anything else, he said, "How long are you in town?" She didn't live in Virginia, but North Carolina, something he was painfully aware of.

Scant hundreds of miles had separated them the past few years, but she might as well have lived on the moon.

"As long as it takes." There was a note of savagery in her tone, which wasn't surprising. The Hailey he'd known once upon a time had been protective of those she'd cared about.

"Where are you staying?"

"Rented a place with my crew."

"Are you just being intentionally vague? Because I'd like to information-share!" he finally snapped. "Easton is missing, and it's my fault." The words tore from his throat, a confession he hadn't told anyone.

To his surprise, she snort-laughed. "There's absolutely no way this is your fault." She was matter-of-fact as her fingers flew over her phone screen, texting someone named Reese—someone she worked with, he knew, from the not-so-thin file he had on her. Yep, he had a file on her like a stalker.

And he wasn't sorry about it.

He was headed to his home in a quiet, historic suburb, and since she hadn't said anything about being dropped off, she was coming with him.

The traffic thinned as he entered the historic district, then the roads grew wider as he pulled into his sprawling neighborhood. Growing up, he'd never imagined he'd live somewhere with triple-paned windows, where all the brick homes had large yards, some had fences or walls, and he had enough space to feel like he was insulated.

"I was supposed to have lunch with Easton yesterday," he said after a few minutes of silence. Not even twenty-four hours had passed, but it felt like an eternity. "But I canceled on him at the last minute because of a meeting. I should have been with him." Jesse's fingers tightened on the wheel, his knuckles turning white.

She gave him a strange look, one he couldn't begin to interpret. "You were supposed to have lunch with him?"

He nodded, the guilt crawling at his throat. If only he'd been there.

She cleared her throat. "That's not your fault. Whoever took him, it's *their* fault. Also I'm pretty sure you're being followed." She glanced in the sideview mirror as she set her phone down. "Two vehicles back, dark SUV with—"

"It's my security."

She glanced over at him again, concern clear on her face. And pathetic as it was, he savored that she actually cared.

"Why do you need security? Is it just because you're rich?"

He laughed lightly at her blunt words. "Yes and no. I normally have security, but after what happened with Easton, I've increased it. He works for me, and what he wanted to talk about was work related so…it just makes sense. So what are you doing over there? Because we both care about Easton, and it makes more sense to information-share. I've given a lot to the Feds, and I'll share it with you too."

She was quiet for a beat, but then nodded. "True. Okay… Wait, where are we going?" She glanced around, as if noticing where they were for the first time. Which didn't surprise him. With her ADHD, she was single-minded sometimes—or more often than not—and ignored extraneous details that didn't interest or concern her.

"My place."

"Oh…" She frowned, then shook her head. "I got a hit on the prints from that asshole. He's a petty thief with a long enough record that I'd call him a career criminal at the ripe age of thirty, but nothing too terrible. The fact that he didn't have a weapon tells me that he didn't want to get slapped with an extra charge if he got caught. This guy is a nobody, but I'm still digging deep into his life to see who his known associates are. Luckily, the cops and Feds have some of that already in the system, so I've got a good starting place. And he knew that either you or I were at Easton's. It's not a coincidence that some jerk broke in after we arrived."

"Yeah, I've been thinking about that. I don't think that guy would have taken me on by himself—not without a weapon. And how would he have known I was going into Easton's place... Unless he knew about our friendship, so I guess that's possible. But I think he was there because he saw you. You're small and unassuming, and he might have wanted to question you."

Or worse. Something Jesse didn't need to voice aloud.

She just grunted, then said, "It's a theory at least. The back of Easton's condo faces a river, so if someone was watching... Hell. They could have had a camera in the condo already. I didn't do a scan or anything."

"I don't think so. His place has been locked down ever since he was taken, and until this afternoon—when you messed with the cameras—we haven't had any issues with his security system."

"So wait, do you own the building or something?"

"Yep."

"Oh. That didn't come up when I did a search of the place."

He lifted a shoulder. "You didn't do a deep enough dive."

"So what's he working on? I couldn't find out too much because your security is tighter than the Feds'."

"He's working on a couple things, namely research on Alzheimer's and ALS. His focus is ALS, but he's working fairly closely with the scientist in charge of the Alzheimer's research. They all collaborate together, and I just give them the money they need and stay out of their way." He wanted to invest in making the world a better place.

"Wow."

"What?"

"Just...I don't know. I didn't realize you were involved with that kind of research."

"You thought I was just another rich asshole?"

"Honestly, I've tried not to think about you at all over the years." Hurt reverberated in her words, striking him right in the chest as he sifted through them.

As he breathed in through the pain, he wasn't sure how to respond. Luckily he didn't need to because as he turned down his street, she let out a low whistle.

The homes got larger the farther he drove. And yeah, some days he struggled with guilt over the type of home he owned, how much he made. But he also gave back a hell of a lot, so he told himself to get over it.

"What do you need to find Easton?" he asked, forcing the words out. He wanted to focus on things he could actually do to help. "My money, my everything is at your disposal. I've already reached out to some contacts, but I'll give you whatever you need."

"Right now I don't need anything except information. And if we're going to work together, my crew is working with me. I work for—"

"Redemption Harbor Security." Yeah, he knew that.

She cleared her throat. "Oh, so what do you know about them?"

"That they recruited you a few years ago when you got out of the Marines, and now you're heading up their North Carolina division. You started that one from the ground up. That you're more or less a private investigative firm slash offshoot of the original Redemption Harbor Consulting in South Carolina." He also knew they were funded by a billionaire and had a few ex-spies or former military types working for them. "Full disclosure, I also might have tried to poach Nova Yates a few years ago."

She shot him a horrified look as he steered down his long drive. "From Gage?"

"What...no! From the company. Jesus. She's got a great reputation, and I ran into her at some stupid gala I'd been forced into and offered her a job. Figured something positive should come out of the night."

Hailey cackled. "I bet Gage threatened your balls."

"You're not wrong about that." Then the cofounder, Skye Arévalo-Stuart, had swiped a real estate purchase out from under him and sent him a "friendly" note that if he came after her people again, he'd lose more than that. Curious, he'd done a little digging into them and liked what he'd found. "I'm not surprised they recruited you. You're amazing," he said as he pulled into the multi-car garage attached to his home.

She made a sort of strangled sound, but he got out and shut the door behind him without looking at her. Something about her had always pulled the truth from him. And if he was being brutally honest with himself, he needed to face reality; he needed closure. Because it had been more than nine years, and he *still* hadn't moved on. It didn't matter how much time had passed, how much he'd accomplished, she was woven into the fabric of his being.

And he needed to figure out a way to move on from her. To do that, he needed to figure out where the hell things had gone wrong all those years ago.

CHAPTER 4

*—True friendship isn't about being there when it's convenient;
it's about being there when it's not.—*

Hailey looked up at Jesse, tried to ignore the way her heart rate couldn't seem to get back to normal around him. It was like it had jumped the track and was now off-roading and out of control, heading toward a deadly cliff's edge. His blue eyes were liquid fire right now as he glared at his employee who'd just asked her to open her backpack to search. The man had also wanted to do a quick pat down.

"No." Jesse practically growled the word as he stared hard at the security guy in his kitchen.

Whew, the energy rolling off him was something else. "It's fine. He can check my stuff." She set her backpack on the huge island countertop. It would be a little humiliating for Jesse to realize she'd stolen a picture from Easton's, but she'd survive the embarrassment.

"Not necessary. No one searches her or touches her, *ever*. Got it? And I don't need any security in the house right now." Jesse's voice held an edge.

But the security guy didn't seem perturbed, just nodded once at the two of them and headed out of the kitchen. A few moments later she heard the alarm on the front door ding open, then closed.

"That was kind of rude." Hailey sat at the island. "I thought you were going to knock his teeth in," she said, shaking her head. "So if we're going to work together," she continued, not expecting any kind of response at his weird behavior, "I'm going to need my own laptop, my things, my tools. And are you sure you want to team up?"

"Of course I'm sure. It makes more sense for us to work together. And you'll just stay here. There's no sense in us being separated or going back and forth to your rental. And I'm sure I've got more space anyway."

Well, he wasn't wrong. "That seems—"

"Like the fastest way to find Easton. And that's the only thing that matters right now."

She couldn't exactly argue with that. And the most needy, desperate part of her didn't want to argue. She liked being around Jesse because apparently she was a masochist. It reminded her of everything she'd lost. But looking around his place, it was clear she'd made the right choice to walk away. He was better off without her. A massively successful entrepreneur, he'd created a handful of apps that had all gone viral, and she'd have just held him back. The killer mansion she was in right now was proof of that.

"Okay, you're right," she said. "And I can admit when I need help. I need to understand more about what Easton was working on, who stood to benefit the most from his current project, or any upcoming projects, if he has any violent exes or just concerning exes in general. I've found a couple exes on social media with no records, but you have an inside view of Easton's life. I want to know anything that could help us, and we'll work from there. My team is wrapping up something now, but we're all ready to find Easton." The words all came out in a rush. "I also need to know more about his life in general, where he hangs out, his habits, everything."

And she hated that she didn't know those things for herself. Something else she could file under "life regrets."

Jesse just stared at her for a long moment, but then the little alarm from the front door dinged, followed by a robotic voice telling them the front door had opened.

She frowned, but Jesse didn't seem worried as he glanced at his phone screen. Maybe it was his security or...a girlfriend. She swallowed hard at that, but before the thought could take root and congeal inside her, Cash Pierce stepped into the kitchen, looking more handsome than should be humanly possible, even with the dark circles under his eyes.

"I thought Jesse was screwing with me," he murmured, crossing the distance to her.

She was already off her stool, shedding years of self-preservation at the sight of one of her oldest, best friends. A man she'd never felt an ounce of attraction to, not like the hunger she felt for Jesse, so maybe that was what made it easier to let her guard down. To pretend that everything was okay for a fraction in time as she threw her arms around him. It was safe to hug Cash because he couldn't break her heart.

Unlike Jesse.

If she let that man touch her, she was terrified she'd fracture into a million pieces and never manage to put herself back together. She'd never recovered from leaving him before; she couldn't do that to herself again.

"It's been too long," Cash murmured, his big arms tightening around her in that familiar, brotherly way she'd missed for far too long.

Stupid tears pricked her eyes, so she buried her face against his chest to banish them. If she let the floodgates open now, she'd never stop it. And these tears weren't for just Easton, they were for all the years she'd lost. All the years she'd forced herself not to look into her former family. The family who'd continued to send her care packages month after month while she'd been in Afghanistan. It didn't matter that she'd never responded, they'd kept sending them. As if she deserved them.

Of all the people she'd expected to abandon her, it was them, since she'd cut them out first. But they'd kept on loving her even when she didn't deserve it.

She pulled back slightly at a rumbling sound, then realized Jesse was right next to them, not so gently shoving Cash back.

"You've hugged long enough, and we have work to do." A simmering anger peeked out of those ice-blue eyes as he stared Cash down.

And Cash, who'd never had a sense of self-preservation, just grinned. Though his smile dimmed almost immediately. "So what happened today? You just said Hailey was back."

"Jesse can explain everything while I grab my stuff. Can I borrow your vehicle?" She held out her hand, already knowing he'd give her the keys to whatever he was driving. She had a few programs running on her laptop back at the rental in her search for Easton, but she needed her things.

Mostly, she needed to get a grip on her sanity.

Cash tossed his keys to her without question, even as Jesse glared in annoyance.

"Fill him in," she said as she scooped up her backpack. "I'll be back." The need to get some distance from Jesse burrowed into her as she practically ran out of his house.

Like a coward.

***

"So what the hell is going on?" Cash rubbed a hand over his face, his normally easygoing expression tight.

"Hailey's helping us out. She was at Easton's—she broke in, was there when I arrived—but she hadn't been there too long. She found a hidden laptop and then bear-sprayed an intruder. Oh, and she's going to be staying here until we find Easton." If she actually came back. For all Jesse knew, she'd ditch Cash's Audi somewhere, and he'd never see her again.

Though, no, because this time he wasn't letting her walk away. He'd hunt her ass down to Siberia if necessary.

Cash blinked once. Twice. "Shit. Okay, then. I just got back from the investigator's place, and he seems useless. What do the Feds have?"

"Not much. Or at least not much that they're sharing. Hailey grabbed the fingerprints of the guy from Easton's and ran them, is looking into known associates. She texted me a list of names... Should I send them to the investigator? Is he really useless, or is this your exhaustion talking?" He and Cash had hired someone to look into Easton's kidnapping because they weren't just going to trust law enforcement.

Cash lifted a shoulder. "I honestly don't know. He was apathetic, and yeah, maybe it's my exhaustion. I don't know and don't care. I didn't like the guy."

"Fine, I'm cutting him loose," Jesse said as he pulled out his cell phone. They'd hired a well-known outfit in DC that came highly recommended, but he was going to trust Cash's gut—he wasn't nicknamed Cash for no reason. And Jesse always trusted the man's gut. "We'll officially hire Redemption Harbor Security for this."

Cash lifted an eyebrow. "You're assuming she'll take your money."

"I'm going straight to her boss," he murmured even as he texted the owner of the company he was cutting loose.

We no longer require your services. Send me your final invoice. Thank you.

Immediately after sending, he called Skye Arévalo-Stuart directly, figuring it was a fifty-fifty of her answering. Hailey might run the North Carolina division, but Skye was one of the founders of Redemption Harbor Consulting. And according to all his research, Skye made most of the final decisions. He'd once heard the phrase "wrangler of dumbasses" thrown around in relation to her.

"Mr. Jesse Lennox," she said after three rings.

"Mrs. Arévalo-Stuart," he said politely. "I'd like to hire Hailey West and her team to officially investigate the kidnapping of Easton Reed. She's already in the DC/Virginia area," he added when there was nothing but silence.

"She's already looking for him for free. She's taken a leave of absence and has the full support and funds of Redemption Harbor Consulting and our security division."

Well, that would have been nice to know, but he managed to pivot. "I didn't know if I should hire her officially for legal reasons. Money is no object." Not something he normally said, but they knew who he was and his net worth.

There was another beat of silence. "I'll need to speak to her first, but, yes, I think it would be best if she's officially hired in an investigative capacity, especially with the Feds involved. We'll draw up a standard contract. Also, I'm sorry about your friend. Easton Reed has a solid reputation, and I respect the work he's doing."

"His reputation is earned," Jesse said around the sudden tightness in his throat.

Easton hadn't been gone long, and someone had specifically taken him. Not killed him when they'd had the chance. Which meant whoever had kidnapped him off the street didn't want him dead. Otherwise, they'd have just put a bullet in him and been done with it. It was something Jesse had to keep reminding himself of as the fear for his childhood friend wanted to drown him. Because he'd seen the video—the kidnapping had been quick and professional. No unnecessary violence. There was a reason behind this; they just needed to find out what the hell it was.

So he could save his younger brother.

"And thank you," he continued. "I know we have a...history." He didn't know what else to call it.

"Trying to poach one of my best employees is no big deal compared to the other shit we face. You've got a solid rep too, and Hailey said you and Cash are good people. It's the only reason I'm agreeing to this at all." Then she disconnected without another word.

Okay, then.

"So Hailey's officially hired?" Cash was pulling food out of the fridge.

"Yep. What are you doing?"

"She's probably going to be hungry for dinner, and so is her team. And I know we could just order something, but I feel absolutely useless right now so I'm going to cook. This never should have happened." Cash started rummaging in the pantry next. He'd been rudderless the past six months. He had a billion-dollar construction company but didn't seem engaged in anything. It was like he'd simply been working to stay busy.

"No shit."

"So she bear-sprayed some guy?" Cash asked after a few beats, his mouth curving up slightly at the corners.

The ice casing around Jesse's heart cracked as he half smiled. "Yeah, even had goggles to protect her face. The woman was prepared."

"So it's definitely not her first time bear-spraying someone," Cash said around a laugh, even if his expression went right back to that worried one. "I've missed her, man."

"Yeah, your hug sure made that clear." Irrationally annoyed, Jesse pulled out the laptop Hailey had found and decided to try breaking the password. He knew Easton well and figured it wouldn't hurt to give it a shot. To do *something*.

"Jesus, I forgot what you were like with her," Cash murmured.

"I'm not *like* anything. You were just mauling her, and it was revolting." Aaaaand he had to stop thinking about that hug, or he'd try to take off the head of his best friend. His brother in everything but blood.

"So…did she hug you?" Cash shot him a mischievous look.

"Get bent."

"I'll take that as a no."

Jesse ignored him as he got to work.

Cash just sniffed imperiously because of course he did. *Handsome bastard.*

CHAPTER 5

—Don't fake being okay.—

"You're being awfully quiet," Reese murmured, her pink-streaked, otherwise jet-black hair pulled back into a high ponytail.

"Just researching," Hailey murmured, her eyes glued to her laptop as Reese drove Cash's Audi like a demon escaping from the bowels of hell. "And we're going to get a ticket if you're not careful."

And probably get arrested or detained because this vehicle certainly wasn't under either of their names. But she was still glad her friend and coworker—aka partner in crime—was driving, because as a rule, Hailey hated it.

"Bullshit, you're the queen of multitasking." Reese took a sharp turn as she sped through a yellow(ish) light.

"Jesus, Reese, I'm gonna hurl if you don't slow down," Elijah grumbled from the back seat.

Hailey wasn't even sure how he fit back there comfortably given his size, but he'd insisted that she sit up front. Because of course he did. Their team was larger than the three of them, but they'd decided to come to Virginia alone since the others were all working on cases. If they needed backup in the form of their actual security team, Hailey knew all she had to do was reach out to the rest of her crew, men she'd served with in Afghanistan and South America and trusted with her life.

"Just setting up an online board of all we have and don't have so I can quickly lay it out for Cash and Jesse." Jesse's name stuck in her throat, but she moved past it. She could admit that she was shaken to her core at seeing him again. Being so near she could reach out and touch him, taste him. Over the years, she'd convinced herself that she'd made up his attractiveness in her head. But if anything, he was more gorgeous than she remembered. Not that it was the reason she'd fallen for him.

Though her fifteen-year-old hormones at the time had certainly enjoyed his looks. But no, it was the way he was a protector, had always looked out for her right from the start. And not just her, but everyone. It was like he had this compulsion to take care of people, to root for the underdog. Cash was the exact same way, though his personality was a lot more relaxed than Jesse's.

"So, I'm not downplaying your missing friend, but are your other friends hot?" Reese's voice was light and teasing as she took another turn, practically tipping them over.

Okay, maybe that was an exaggeration, but there were horns honked, and Hailey had to grab the "oh shit" handle so she didn't fall over into the console. "They're good-looking." She paused, glanced at her gorgeous friend, felt an unfamiliar spike of jealousy stab into her middle, sink in deep, take hold like tree roots. "But if you make a move on Jesse, you'll wake up one morning without all that pretty hair."

Reese gave her a startled look, then sputtered out a surprised laugh. "Savage. And I believe you, so duly noted. Besides, I wouldn't want to hook up with some asshole billionaire anyway. But no shade if you do."

"Look at the road!" Elijah shouted from the back.

"It's out there," Reese grumbled as she slowed down for the neighborhood turnoff. Then she let out a low whistle. "Might be worth losing my hair—"

"I swear to all that is holy, Reese!"

Her friend cackled manically as she slowed to a decent speed. "I'm just playing around, but you definitely downplayed whatever happened with you and Mr. Billionaire."

"No shit," Elijah murmured from the back.

"For the record," Reese continued, "I really was kidding. I wouldn't do anything to lose you as a friend."

"I know. You're just a dick sometimes."

Reese snickered. "True enough. So, my parents have money, but this is like next-level." She let out another whistle as she eyed the historic neighborhood that housed actual former presidents.

Even Elijah, who was never impressed by anything, made a sort of grunt as Reese steered down the long driveway to Jesse's brick monstrosity. The gate had been left open, but she had a feeling Jesse kept it closed normally.

"What's up with the security?" Reese asked.

Hailey eyed the two men in dark suits on the front porch and knew there were more people they couldn't see. Not to mention all the cameras she'd seen and more she knew she hadn't. "I think it might have something to do with Easton's kidnapping, but I'm not sure." She was going to find out, however. "Also, I found something strange, but we'll talk about it once we're inside." She shut her laptop, ignored Reese's curious look as her friend jerked the vehicle to a halt.

"Let me out before I actually do hurl," Elijah groaned.

Hailey moved quickly, jumping out and moving the seat forward in seconds. Elijah tumbled out even before Reese was out of the driver's seat.

Cash and Jesse strode out of the palatial home, Cash frowning at Reese as he approached. "Are you the lunatic who was driving my car? I got an alert on my phone that you got up to a hundred."

"Jesus, I knew I wasn't crazy," Elijah muttered before he went to the trunk, grabbed his small duffel.

"What's the point in having a car like this if you don't drive it like it's stolen?" Reese tossed him the keys then turned to Jesse, effectively dismissing Cash. "I'm Reese, Hailey's bestie. And I'm sorry about your friend. We're going to find him."

Jesse blinked, then murmured his thanks before he moved to the trunk and started grabbing their bags—which weren't many. They all packed light for the most part, except Reese, who had a small bag just for her hair products.

"I've cleared out some extra room in my office for your gear. I work from home a lot and have a big space and likely all the tech you'll need," he said as he lifted Hailey's bag.

She went to take it from him, but he simply sidestepped her.

So Hailey let it go and tried not to admit that she liked him carrying her things. It almost felt like he was making a statement, but she was probably projecting. "I might have found something," she said as she followed after him, the others not far behind. "Not sure yet, but I'll know soon."

"I managed to get past the password on Easton's laptop, but all the files are encrypted." Frustration practically vibrated from Jesse as they headed down a long hallway.

She noticed that none of the security had looked twice at any of them since they'd parked, so he must have told them that her people were fine too. He was putting a lot of trust in her, considering they hadn't seen each other in almost a decade. That knowledge did something to her she didn't want to acknowledge—and it wormed its way into a little crack in her heart. "I'm impressed you got through his encryption at all."

"I didn't, actually. Not in the way you do it. I just figured out his password. It was a combination of the address we all lived in when we were kids and the street name."

Oh. *Oooooh.* Hailey's throat went tight as she tried to shove aside all her emotions. But the lid had popped off, and all those feelings she'd been effectively—*ish*—ignoring for years bubbled over the side.

Unable to speak, she simply followed him, half listening to the other three behind them. Cash was apparently annoyed by Reese's driving and wasn't letting it go, which was fair. As Hailey stepped into the office with Jesse, she forgot about everything for a moment as she took in the space.

There were two huge screens on one wall, and on another, built-in bookshelves encased two huge windows overlooking his lush backyard. A desk that was clearly his sat near the window, but there were a couple others strategically placed near the wall screens she guessed his employees used when they were here working.

There was also a coffee bar and a separate seating area next to an electric fireplace. The man had certainly made a killing through work, so it made sense that his home office reflected it, but she was still impressed. Especially since it didn't feel cold, but actually lived in. And the art was... well, it was sort of weird and beautiful at the same time. Various animals in shades of gray had a bright rainbow of paint dripping down on them in each painting.

"Holy shit," Reese murmured, looking around. "This is as good as our office."

"Maybe better." Elijah moved up next to Hailey, and she didn't miss the way Jesse's eyebrows drew together.

As if he was annoyed that she was standing so close to another man. He'd been protective and, okay, possessive, when they'd been younger. But he couldn't *still* be that way about her anymore. Right? Oh, no. And she shouldn't like that he was. She was here for one reason and one reason only.

"Oh, shit," Cash muttered, right before she heard a thud then a muted breaking sound. "Sorry."

Hailey turned to find that he'd knocked her backpack off one of the desks. "It's fine." She hurried over to pick it up, but he was faster. "I've got it," she said, but he waved her away as he opened up the back zipper.

"Hope what I broke wasn't important."

"It's nothing, I swear." She tried to tug her pack from him, but Cash was annoyingly large and refused to budge as he started pulling out the broken pieces of the frame she'd stolen.

Hopefully, he wouldn't pull out the frame or picture—okay, too late. He'd discovered her thievery. "Where'd you get this?" He dropped the busted frame into a nearby wastebasket, but held the photograph up by two fingers.

Thankfully Elijah and Reese were setting up their laptops and oohing and ahhing over Jesse's sleek wall screens.

She grabbed it out of Cash's hand and held it to her chest as both he and Jesse stared down at her. "I stole it from Easton's place," she muttered, ignoring their gazes—or trying to.

But she felt the heat of Jesse's eyes on her even as she turned away and pulled her own laptop out of its protective sleeve. She wanted to start digging into what she'd just found before they'd arrived here, see if it warranted further investigation. Not talk about a picture that meant nothing. *Nothing*.

"Klepto Hailey is back," Cash snorted, delight in his voice.

"Whatever," she muttered. "That was one time, and it was a freaking Mars bar. I'm not a klepto. And I didn't have a picture of all of us, and I took it on impulse. Don't be a butthead."

Cash snorted again, but it morphed into a disbelieving laugh. "Pretty sure you're the only person ever to call me a butthead."

"Then people are calling you that behind your back," Reese said without turning around from where she'd settled next to Elijah.

Cash turned a speculative look in her direction before he moved to the other side of the huge space, leaving Hailey with Jesse as she turned her computer back on. "Can I hook into that screen?" she asked, nodding at the wall screen similar to one they used for jobs back at their office.

His expression was unreadable, but he nodded before he told her how to log in and sync up with his system.

For the next ten minutes, the three of them set up their laptops, each claiming one of the wall screens. Jesse, for his part, sat next to her quietly, still working on the laptop she'd found at Easton's. He might not be as expert at her at hacking, but he had more than decent skills when it came to breaking into things. Still, he was more of a creator, always had been. It was why his apps had done so well. Or part of the reason. He had vision, but also follow-through and an understanding of what people wanted.

"Okay, so this is what I found on the way over here," Hailey said into the quiet, only glancing at Reese's and Elijah's screens momentarily. Reese was doing a deep dive into Easton's social medias, and Elijah was helping her.

Hailey pulled up the bank accounts she'd stumbled across because of a very messy trail. Almost as if the person who'd set it up wanted it to be found.

"That's not where Easton banks." Jesse frowned as he looked at the screen.

"I know, and I don't think this is his account. It was just set up in the past fifteen hours. Right before or during his kidnapping. It's weird. Now look at this." A few other tabs popped up, and she clicked on them so that they were side by side. "This random account pops up under his name after being funded from who knows where—I'll figure it out though, mark my word. And now deposits are going out to overseas accounts." Her fingers moved over her keyboard quickly. "Two of these accounts are flagged by Interpol for suspected terrorism. Someone wants it to look like Easton is dumb enough to fund terrorism. And they might have gotten away with it if there hadn't been video of him being kidnapped."

"Whoever this is could still try that angle," Jesse murmured.

She nodded, biting back her frustration. "Yeah, anything is possible at this point." And they didn't know enough, aka they knew jack shit, about who'd taken him.

"That won't stand up to a deep inspection." Reese had swiveled in her chair as she eyed the accounts Hailey had shared directly with her.

"Maybe not, but I doubt anyone expected you to find this so quickly," Jesse said.

"Or maybe they're doing this to throw suspicion on his kidnapping," Cash added. "Maybe they're assuming the FBI will find the account and question the authenticity of his abduction."

Hailey's gut tightened at the thought. Not that she had much faith in the Feds anyway, but she still wanted them focused on figuring out who'd taken Easton. They had vast resources, and when they weren't bogged down by bureaucracy, they could get shit done.

"We could shut down the account and follow the money," Hailey murmured. She was going to follow the money no matter what, but they could also basically erase the account and erase any link to Easton. He wasn't around to defend himself, and it pissed her off that someone was trying to make him look dirty.

She looked at Jesse, then Cash. "What do you guys think?" She didn't want to screw up the FBI investigation, but if they found this, she worried it would divert their resources.

"Shut it down, or at least make it so the Feds can't find it. I don't want to muddy the waters when they're trying to locate him." Jesse's voice was icy, his thought process clearly the same as hers.

Cash nodded in agreement.

Okay, then.

As they got to work, Jesse pulled up his own laptop. "What can I do to help?"

"Tell me about Easton's current work. I know you've gone over this with the Feds, but tell me about his coworkers."

"I've already got a file on all that. I can send it to you."

"Okay, yeah, send me info on everyone he works with personally."

"I'll do one better. I'll send you a file on everyone who works in the building with him. Everyone is thoroughly vetted and then their financials are randomly checked a couple times during the year—they all know this when they're employed—but I know that nothing is foolproof. I've already reached out to the company I use to vet potential hires to do deeper dives on current employees."

"We'll still look into them, but thanks. This is gold." She didn't look up from her computer except to give him a small smile.

As she started working on shutting down the bank account, she lost track of time and only blinked when Jesse set a mug of hot peppermint tea in front of her.

She looked up at him. "What's this?"

"Tea. And Cash cooked earlier. You all need to eat. Take ten or fifteen minutes to recharge." He looked at the three of them, but his gaze lingered on her the longest.

"He's right, we should eat," Reese said as she stretched. "I don't think you even ate breakfast. And I know you didn't eat lunch."

Oh, right. "I got a latte at that coffee shop," Hailey grumbled, feeling defensive.

"Well, I cooked chicken and eggplant parm," Cash said, throwing an arm around her.

"Eggplant parm!" Reese practically sprinted past them on her way to the kitchen, making Hailey laugh.

Hailey hugged Cash back. "My girl loves food."

"Noted." There was a glint in his eyes, taking her by surprise as he looked in the direction Reese had gone.

"No way." She pinched his side. "Don't even think about it."

He gave her a cheeky grin, but it was overshadowed by the worry in his dark eyes. "No promises."

Even though Hailey hated to stop working, she understood that they needed to recharge. And she had multiple programs running simultaneously doing financial and social media searches on Easton's coworkers. If they could at least narrow down a reason for his kidnapping, it would be the starting point they needed.

As she stepped into the kitchen, she realized that either Cash or Jesse had already set up plates and food family-style at the island. And the rich scents had her stomach rumbling as she approached.

"Sit, I'll plate your food," Jesse murmured to her, sending warmth curling through her.

At a loss for words, and okay, beyond exhausted, she slid onto one of the high-top stools. That was when she realized it was after nine.

"I didn't realize how late it was." Reese slid onto the stool next to her, mirroring her thoughts.

"Me neither. Maybe after we eat, we get a few hours of sleep." When working on a job, she often slept erratically, grabbing a couple hours here and there.

"I need to wrap up the Urichko job." Reese's eyes went a little feral at that, but then they lit up as Cash set a plate of food in front of her. "Thanks, boo," she said teasingly before she turned away from him.

But Hailey saw the heated look from Cash, the one with clear curiosity and interest. Too bad for him, her friend only dated aimless losers with no ability to take care of themselves. She wasn't even sure if she'd call what Reese had relationships—they never lasted long enough.

"Here." Jesse slid a plate in front of her, along with a salad and her favorite dressing, then held out two wine bottles. Both expensive labels. "Red or white?"

"Ah, red, please. And thanks," she added lightly before digging into her food—and avoiding his hot gaze.

Why was he looking at her like that? She couldn't even begin to describe the look, but she felt the heat of it scorching all the way to her toes. He was watching her as if he could see right through to her very soul. As if...he was maybe remembering what she looked like naked. Well she thought about him naked from time to time. Or more than that.

"So what's the Urichko job?" Cash asked as he took a seat across from them, his own plate piled high with food.

"Ah..." Hailey looked at the others. They weren't supposed to talk about their jobs, but this one wasn't on the books. "Normally, we wouldn't be able to say anything..."

"But we're doing this one for free," Reese added, grinning all feral rage now. "And the short of it is, some bitch who hates kids and has no business teaching is about to lose her job because of what we found on her. Elijah found it actually," she nodded at their friend.

He shrugged and grinned. "Got lucky with this one."

Hailey just shook her head. "He's full of it," she said to Jesse and Cash. "We couldn't find anything concrete on this teacher other than she 'resigned' from a few schools and only got her current job because she's related to the principal through marriage."

"We were spinning our wheels," Reese picked up where Hailey left off. "So Elijah reached out to his mom, who was a guidance counselor, and it's like she's tapped into this network of badasses."

Elijah laughed lightly. "She reached out to a lot of contacts and finally found a friend of a friend who passed her some information that was never digitized. This particular teacher likes to target kids with disabilities. And it's never been provable shit—until now."

"What are you guys going to do?" Cash asked after swallowing a mouthful.

Hailey wasn't sure how the man ate so much food and looked so fit.

At that thought, she stole a peek at Jesse, found him staring at her, unabashedly. And he didn't look away, just pinned her with those ice-blue eyes, held fast.

What was he trying to do to her? She swallowed hard, and like the coward she was, she broke eye contact first and looked back as Reese said, "We're still debating if we want to post the video we have of her on social media anonymously, or send her what we have anonymously and tell her to retire immediately."

"Why are you going after her? Who brought her to your attention?" Jesse asked, that delicious voice drawing her gaze back to him.

"Ah, a friend of ours has a Deaf daughter—who goes to a school for the Deaf and Hard of Hearing. And she's part of a small community with other Deaf kids online. One of her friends at a different school told her about this teacher who's been hassling her and how it feels targeted. But also, how she can't prove it. Basically, this teacher is gaslighting her and just generally being an awful human being. And now we have a very short video of her talking shit to another teacher about one of her students, but it cuts off before it's too, *too* awful. But we also have some written complaints from parents over the years. Again, nothing too terrible at face value, but when you look at the pattern of behavior..." Hailey shrugged. "She's a shitty human who doesn't need to be teaching kids at all."

"How old is the video?" Jesse asked.

"Ah, like fifteen years old and a little grainy. The only thing holding me back is that she specifically names a student in the video, and I don't know that we have the right to blast something like that where a teacher specifically mocks a kid. That kid is an adult now, but this could dredge up... I don't know, I'm torn. It could put this former student in the spotlight if the video goes viral. What would you guys do?"

Cash cleared his throat. "If the end goal is to get her to retire, send it to her, demand that she does. She'll make the decision for you. If she doesn't think it's bad enough for her to retire, then go ahead and post it. She'll either weather the storm or not—let the public decide. Or just anonymously send it to the student she mocked, and let *her* decide. The kid is now an adult and she's the wronged person. One of many, it sounds like. Maybe the decision should be hers."

"You're not cutthroat enough," Reese murmured. "I'll let you see the video, then you answer, okay?"

Cash just gave her a cheeky grin.

"What about you? What would you do?" Reese asked Jesse.

Jesse just shrugged, but didn't respond.

Hailey cut off a piece of her eggplant. "He'd go full-on scorched earth." Because her man—ah, *former*—hated bullies. Jesus, had she just thought of him as hers? She really did need sleep.

"Seriously?" Reese looked between the two of them.

Jesse just lifted a shoulder again, but this time it was in agreement with Hailey. Yeah, some things hadn't changed.

CHaPTer 6

—Sometimes hope is the only thing that keeps us going.—

Easton cracked his eyes open, fought the roil of nausea as he tried to sit up.

A hint of light peeked in through the slit in one of the curtains... A street light maybe, not natural light.

He was afraid to open his eyes any wider, to make any movement in case someone was in the room with him. So he listened, trying to keep his breathing steady, even. As if he were still asleep.

After a few more minutes, when he didn't hear anyone else breathing, he opened his eyes wider and tried to sit up. One of his wrists was cuffed to the frame of the bed, so all he could do was half rise and look around as he rolled onto his side and managed to scoot up a bit.

Wincing at the pain in his wrist and fighting another sweep of nausea, he managed to swing his legs off the side of the bed and move closer to the top of the frame so he wasn't so hunched over trying to sit up.

The bedroom looked the same, so at least they hadn't moved him. He scanned the room as best he could with the muted light coming in from the bathroom. Two windows, high and wide, both covered by thick curtains. Crown molding, a closet, and an attached bathroom. Some kind of light was emanating from the bathroom, but it didn't seem bright enough to be overhead lights.

But the house was fairly new, given the wood flooring and the modern tile and layout he could see in the bathroom. He cataloged everything he could in case he had to remember it for the police. No, not in case.

When he recounted it to the police.

Because he was going to get out of here. His friends would come for him. His brothers in everything except blood. Cash and Jesse, and probably Hailey too. More out of guilt for her, but he didn't care.

He wanted to get out of this shithole. After spending years in crappy foster homes, only to find his best friends, his family, at the last one, to create a good life for himself, he refused to die in this place.

He tugged on the cuff, then felt around the top of the bedframe for a screw or something that he could maybe remove, loosen one of the bars from the frame. Because he didn't need to get the cuff off, he simply needed to get the cuff off of the frame.

It was too dark to see much, but he ran his fingers over the smoothness, stopped at a couple areas where there was a slightly raised texture. Screws maybe, but they were too small for him to actually turn or loosen.

Fighting the punch of disappointment, he lay back down as another wave of exhaustion swept through him. His feet were cramping and uncomfortable, likely because he was dehydrated. His captors had barely been feeding him or giving him anything to drink. The only silver lining was that he wasn't having to soil himself because his body was desperate to retain water. And okay, he knew they didn't want him dead.

He closed his eyes for a moment, then stretched out, shoving at the curtain with his foot. Luckily he was tall, so he managed to push the curtain forward just a bit, allowing more light into the room, onto the bare mattress he'd been dumped on.

With no blanket.

Which was just icing on the crap cake of his day. He didn't think it had been a full twenty-four hours, but he could have lost more track of time than he'd realized.

He was supposed to have had lunch with Jesse...and Hailey. He hadn't told either of them that he'd invited the other. Which in hindsight probably hadn't been the smartest thing to spring on both of them.

But it had been almost ten years, and he didn't give a shit. Life was too short, and he'd decided to force them to meet up, to see each other again.

And maybe get over their bullshit. Though the blame really fell on Hailey's shoulders, even if he understood why she'd cut them out. He seemed to be the only one who did.

Jesse had bailed on him first, then Hailey had sent an apology text saying that she was tied up for work. So he'd decided to walk home instead of taking a Lyft, and two assholes in a van had kidnapped him.

It had happened so fast, and even though he'd managed to run, they'd been faster. He shuddered as he remembered feeling powerless as someone had shoved something over his head. Then he'd felt the prick of a needle in his neck, and...nothing.

Until he'd woken up here. At least there had been a couple fruit bars on the bed the first time he'd woken up. And a small water bottle.

Now his wrapper and empty bottle remained so he didn't think anyone had been by to check on him. And it was so quiet that he wondered if...

Had he just been left here to die?

Ice slid through his veins, and he started to tremble as he curled up on his side as best he could. He pulled in a breath, trying to remain calm, to remind himself that he had people who cared for him, who would turn over every rock until he was found.

CHAPTER 7

—Running away from your problems is a race you'll never win.—

Jesse turned at a slight sound and found Hailey standing in the doorway to his office in her pajamas and the thick robe he'd left on the guest bed for her. He tried not to stare. And failed.

"Hey, you can come in," he murmured, turning away from the big window overlooking his pool and backyard. It was dark out, but there were enough lights illuminating the pool and yard to see. Even if he had been more or less zoning out.

"I didn't realize anyone was awake. I just wanted to check on the programs I have running." She stepped into his office on quiet feet, avoiding his gaze as she sat in front of her and Easton's laptops. She worked on his first, frowned at it before turning to her own.

"You can come in here any time," he said, moving closer to her, almost against his will. She was a magnet to him, a drug he couldn't get enough of.

And he'd never gotten over her. That much was clear as he looked at the sharp lines of her jaw and profile. She frowned at the screen, scrunched her nose up in frustration before she sat back. "I hate waiting," she grumbled, sounding more like the Hailey he'd known years ago.

Not the distant woman she'd been since he'd found her in Easton's condo. He pulled up a chair and sat next to her, but not so close that he'd crowd her and make her run.

Something she was an expert at.

"I got some responses from my employment investigator, forwarded everything to you and the others," he said into the quiet. "I've already taken a few people off the list of potential suspects."

She rubbed her fingers against the side of her temples. "Yeah, I saw it pop up. Your investigator is fast. At least we can take some people out of the equation."

"And you managed to mask that bank account."

"Yeah." Her tone was frustrated, something he understood. "For now. The Feds still might find the bogus account."

"Whoever took him wants him alive," he said, for himself or her, he wasn't sure. Maybe both. "Otherwise they'd have just killed him on the street."

"I keep telling myself that too." Her voice was soft as she finally met his gaze, her tawny brown eyes unreadable.

And he could feel the pulse in the air, that thick electricity that had always been there between them. Right from the beginning. Even when she'd put up her fists as if she wanted to fight him, he'd been knocked on his ass from the force of her. She had a wildness in her he loved, wouldn't mind drowning in. "So how's it been since settling back stateside?"

She blinked in surprise, but lifted a shoulder. "Well, anything is better than living in a war zone. For the most part I was lucky, that being a relative word. My specialty was Intel so I wasn't on the front lines, but our base was bombed more than once. I...it was hard to sleep. Though to be fair, it's hard to sleep most days now too," she murmured, rubbing at her temples again.

"Is that how you were hired by Redemption Harbor? I know some of them were in the military."

"Ah, no, that's not how. Not directly anyway. All the founders are older than me. Than all of us; Reese and Elijah and all the others back in North Carolina. But the man I worked under knew Skye from something long ago, and when I told him I was getting out, he put me in contact with her. And that was that." She eyed him speculatively for a moment. "That was bold reaching out to her today."

He didn't make a habit of half-assing anything or holding back. He saw something and went for it. Just as he'd done with Hailey—until she'd left without a backward glance. "I'll do anything to find Easton."

Hailey nodded in understanding, and he could see the shadows lurking in her eyes. The guilt. Something he understood because he felt it too. If he hadn't canceled lunch with Easton none of this would have happened. Or he'd have been with him when it had happened.

Would have been able to protect him and fight back.

"This is a nice robe," she murmured almost absently.

He nodded, his gaze dipping to the lapels that were overlapped and covered everything he wanted to see, unfortunately. Not that he'd forgotten what she looked like naked. Or what she sounded like when she came. Nope. The images and sounds were seared into his psyche and liked to torture him at night.

Or any time he was alone.

"You didn't have to cut us all out," he said into the quiet, because screw it. "Even if you'd wanted to end things with me." He nearly choked on the words, but forced himself to continue. "You didn't have to cut all of us out of your life entirely. We were family." And he still thought of her as family, no matter how messed up that was.

She rubbed a hand over her face, and to his surprise her eyes glittered with unshed tears as she looked away, abruptly stood. "I actually did, for both our sakes," she whispered before striding from the room.

Leaving him alone, wondering what the hell she meant by that.

After a moment, he shoved up as years of anger erupted and boiled over. He followed after her and didn't bother knocking on her door, even though it was a dick thing to do. He barged in as if he had every right.

She turned at the door opening, already taking the robe off to reveal a skimpy pajama set.

He blinked.

"What the hell are you doing?" she demanded, hands on hips, not bothering to cover back up.

He stalked toward her. "I want an answer, Hailey!"

When she flinched, he stopped where he stood but didn't make a move to leave. He would never hurt her, something she had to know, but he'd also never raised his voice.

"No, you don't," she finally snapped, fire in her tawny brown eyes. "You don't want to know anything." Her voice cracked on the last word, and to his horror the sheen of tears he'd seen before were now a floodgate rolling down her cheeks.

Oh no. No, no, no.

His legs were moving before he'd processed it, the need to comfort her overwhelming everything else. Going on instinct, he gathered her into his arms as her petite frame shook with tears. To his surprise, she didn't shove him off her, but instead buried her face against his chest and held him tight.

And cried and cried, her sobs quiet even as her entire body shook.

He'd never seen her cry before. Not once. This was... Hell, he couldn't stand this. He scooped her up and carried her to the huge bed—she was in the guest room right next to his bedroom. Some compulsive part of him had needed her as close as possible. The same part of him that had given her his robe to wear because he'd wanted her in something of his, wanted his scent on her.

He didn't even need to analyze anything to know why. He was possessive and obsessive when it came to her.

Always had been.

He made some sort of soothing sound as he slid into the big bed with her, holding her close. After a while, she stopped shaking, but kept her face buried against his shoulder as she curled into his hold.

"Sorry," she finally murmured, but didn't look at him. Barely moved at all.

"Nothing to be sorry for." He might want answers from her, but not like this. "Just close your eyes." Because he wasn't letting her go, and she needed to sleep.

She inhaled deeply, and he thought she might say something, but instead she made a sort of *hmming* sound that might have been an agreement before she laid her head on his shoulder.

Holding her like this eventually lulled him into a sleep as well. It had been so long since he'd slept holding someone—a little more than nine years to be exact. Having the pressure of her against him, the scent of her surrounding him, his body finally surrendered, and he fell into a deep sleep.

But when he woke up, she was gone.

CHAPTER 8

Nine years ago

Hailey,

I tried your cell but it was disconnected, and you're not answering my email, or even Cash or Easton's emails, so I'm writing a *letter, on paper*. After months, we managed to find out your FPO mailing address and decided to give this a shot. I know I shouldn't put this in a letter when you're God knows where right now, but I'm so angry at you. So pissed that you just left and cut us all out. I know you love me. I know you love all of us! And you just bailed like the past few years meant nothing. I'm also worried for you, and I hate that you're somewhere without all of us watching your back.

I hope the care package makes up for my words, even if I'm not sorry for them. Because I still love you, no matter what. Please write back, even a sentence. I just want to know you're okay. Above all, I hope you're staying safe and that you know you have people back home who love and care about you. That you'll always have a home with us.

Always yours,
Jesse

***

Hey assface,

So you bailed on us without a word? Man, Jesse is so pissed! What the hell, short stuff? We're family and not the toxic kind. The good kind. I know, I know, I should be nicer since you're in...Afghanistan? I don't know, I'm just guessing. It took forever to find your mailing address so I hope this finds you well.

Even though I'm angry at you for abandoning us (imagine my most melodramatic voice right now), I still didn't eat any of your snacks. I feel like that deserves mentioning because it took a vast amount of self-control I didn't know I had. You're welcome, assface. Oh, you don't like that name? Then maybe you write back, or call, or send a carrier pigeon. Anything will do. If you do, I'll upgrade you to butthead.

Oh, so I've been thinking about joining the army. What do you think? I'm going to at least finish getting my associates beforehand though. Maybe. Easton has already finished with his bachelor's and is now working on his master's. Something double science, blah, blah, blah. I don't understand, which means it must be impressive. I can't help but think what would have happened if he'd actually been born into a loving family who supported him instead of being bounced around the system. He'd have probably graduated high school at like twelve and already had his doctorate.

And even though you didn't ask, Jesse is miserable without you. All he ever does is work. He's thrown himself into a new project. An app that's already garnered a lot of interest. So I invested in him. Figured I'm going to throw my limited funds in with a sure thing.

I miss you. And I hope you're staying as safe as possible.

—Cash

***

Hailey,

I hope you're doing well. From what I understand, it's very hot and dry where you are, so I included some snacks I know you like and that will survive the weather. I've also included some books I thought you might find interesting. Words have never been my strong point, but I miss you terribly. You're the first real friend I ever made, and no matter what happens between us, I will always treasure that and you.

I understand that you had to make the right decision for your life, even if I don't understand why. So if you wish for us to stop writing or sending things, please tell us to, and we will. If not, I will continue to send you care packages and letters.

Sincerely,

Easton

CHAPTER 9

—She's all the chaos I need.—

Jesse stepped into the kitchen to find Hailey sitting at the countertop, her laptop in front of her. Cash was leaning against one of the counters with a to-go coffee mug in hand. And that was when Jesse noticed two backpacks on the island top.

"What's going on?"

"I was two minutes away from waking you up," Cash said, giving him a pointed look.

Probably because Jesse looked like he was about to kick his friend's ass. Why the hell hadn't anyone woken him up? It was only seven, but it was clear they'd been awake for a while.

"I found something on Easton's laptop." Hailey moved her laptop over so he could see the screen. "I copied everything to mine because I have more programs. This one of his seems to be a backup more than anything, where he was storing information. One of the files I managed to unencrypt has a bunch of addresses. I started digging into them, and each address is linked back to a big pharma company. One of your competitors."

A little buzz started at the back of his skull. "And?"

"Well, that's it for now. I'm now digging into the company itself. I don't know what these notes next to each address mean. It's in some kind of code I'm guessing only Easton understands," she grumbled in frustration. "We're going to check out some of the addresses because I can't find much using Google Earth. I've got county records from each place, and the taxes are up to date on all of them. But other than that, there's nothing on these locations except some generic websites that look fake as shit to me. Each website is using stock photos and what look like fake employee résumés. If I wasn't looking at them in bulk and I didn't know they were all linked to the same pharma company, it probably wouldn't trigger anything. But something weird is going on. And clearly Easton had this information in an encrypted file for a reason, and maybe that reason is why he was taken. Reese and Elijah are going to check out two in North Carolina."

As if they knew they were being talked about, the two of them strode into the kitchen, dressed and ready. Elijah grabbed one of the backpacks from the countertop. "Thanks for letting us crash here and for the food."

Jesse simply nodded at the man, then pointed at three addresses on her screen. All Kentucky addresses. "These are all fairly close together, and if we use the jet, we can visit each one today."

Hailey frowned, as if she was going to argue.

But he shook his head. "This is the first substantial lead we have. I'm going with you, and you'll get there faster with my plane."

"I'm going too," Cash murmured, his jaw set in determination. "Either with you guys or with Reese and Elijah."

"Uh-uh, you're going with them." Reese's expression was hard.

"Trust me, you don't want to be in the car while she's driving anyway." Elijah's tone was dry as he glanced at Cash.

Jesse pulled out his cell, already calling his pilot as he said, "I'll be ready to go in ten." Then he strode from the room as he set things up on his end.

That buzz he got sometimes in business swarmed through him, telling him this was what they'd been waiting for.

Innovative Labs Inc. was one of his biggest competitors in the STEM division of his business portfolio. He was diversified, the apps he'd created when he'd been young having taken on a life of their own. They'd given him the money to invest in things that mattered, and with the help of Easton and Cash, he'd managed to drive money to worthwhile causes—which in turn ended up creating more jobs and income.

Innovative Labs Inc. had astronomical markups for their medicines, and while he understood the need to make money, to have stability, it shouldn't be at the cost of helping people who needed it the most. Doing that was criminal.

So for his own company's research, he'd given Easton the reins to do what he wanted and thus they were one of the few small R&D companies that was practically giving away their research for nothing. It was in the realm of possibility that Innovative Labs had targeted Easton but...he couldn't figure out why. Or what the hell the addresses on Easton's backup laptop had to do with anything.

***

Hailey didn't want to go anywhere with Jesse, especially not after last night when she'd blubbered all over him until she'd fallen asleep in his arms. He'd always had this magic way—read, *annoying*—of making her open up.

And something had cracked open inside her last night. She was going to blame it on lack of sleep and worry for Easton. So when she'd woken up a couple hours ago, it had taken everything in her to ease off Jesse and run to Reese's room.

Like a coward.

Thankfully she and Reese wore the same size, so she'd grabbed a shower, changed into jeans and a loose sweater and gotten to work.

And now she was stuck on a private plane with Jesse and Cash for the next hour. Cash was on the phone, clearly fielding work calls, and Jesse was doing the same.

Good, let them handle that while she tried to ignore what Jesse's mere presence did to her. Besides, she needed to catch up on work too. And other than the pilot, there was no one else on the plane, thankfully.

She absolutely hated flying, but this was a lot better than going commercial, that was for sure. The interior was basically like a luxury car, but a lot bigger. Quilted, comfortable leather seats, blue inlay lighting, a couple flat screens, a kitchenette, sleek bathroom, and even a small bedroom in the very back. Everything was in light grays and blues, the calming colors perfect for flying.

At least she could lose herself in work for a while, turn off the voice in her brain that wanted to obsess about Jesse on top of everything else.

He'd been so sweet last night, or this morning really, when she'd used him like a tissue. Ugh. No. *Stop thinking about that*, she ordered herself.

She wasn't sure how long she'd been working when Cash dropped into the seat across from her, a sparkling water in hand. He set one next to her on the shiny little built-in table. "You need to drink. It'll help with dehydration when flying."

"Thanks." She knew that. She just got caught up in work sometimes. Okay, *all* the time. She loved her job but knew she could be obsessive. Part of that was from her ADHD and also because she had no real personal life. Sure, she had friends, men and women from the Marines, and others she loved. But she worked to the point of obsession, and deep down, she knew why.

It kept all the voices in her head quiet.

"So, tell me about Reese. She single?"

"Ah..." It took a moment for Hailey's brain to catch up. She shut her laptop as she cleared her throat. "I don't think it matters either way because you're not her type."

He blinked in surprise. "Why not?"

She bit back a grin. Cash was ridiculously good-looking, so yeah, she could understand his reaction. "She usually dates..." Hailey paused and tried to think of a nice way to say *losers who tried to mooch off her*. Reese was this amazing woman, but for some reason had a blind spot when it came to the men she dated. They were all users, where she was a giver. But how could she put that into words? "Um...I don't want to talk about this."

Cash lifted a shoulder, and something gleamed in his eyes as he said, "Okay, let's talk about all the letters and care packages we sent you. I assume you received them, but we never heard back, and I always wondered." He stared at her now, his green eyes piercing.

"Oh, well, we can talk about Reese. So—"

"Nope. Too late. So. Did you receive the packages?"

She glared at Cash for a moment. "I did. Thank you." She glanced over Cash's shoulder, saw Jesse watching them intently from his seat near the back of the plane. He wasn't even pretending not to listen. Sighing, she looked at Cash again. "I appreciate everything you guys sent, and I should have said it sooner. And I'm sorry I never wrote back. It was shitty of me to do."

Cash blinked in surprise. "For real?"

"What?"

"I expected more pushback."

She rubbed her hands over her face, beyond exhausted. The coffee had barely helped after the night she'd had. And all she could think about was Easton, wondering where he was, hoping he was okay. The not knowing was excruciating. "Look, I should have written you guys back. I'm the *worst*, okay?"

"Jesus, that's not what I'm trying to say. You're not the worst."

"You called me assface in most of your letters." Her tone was dry.

In response, Cash grinned, totally unrepentant.

"You what?" Jesse frowned from his seat, sliding his own laptop to the side as he glared at Cash.

"He called me assface. A *lot*."

"She *was* an assface."

Jesse frowned even harder, if that was possible. "Don't call her that."

"You called her worse." Cash glanced over his shoulder so she couldn't see the look he shot Jesse, but Jesse glared at him in response.

Ouch. She shouldn't be surprised, but still. Feeling an unexpected punch of emotions, she picked up her laptop. "I've got some work, so—"

Cash turned back around. "No way. You've got nowhere to go, and I want answers."

"I already answered you."

"We haven't even begun to scratch the surface of the questions I have."

Rolling her eyes, she stood, grabbing her backpack and laptop. She'd rather sit with Jesse and deal with his brooding looks than deal with this crap from Cash.

What more did he want anyway? She'd admitted that she sucked. Why couldn't he just let it go?

"Running again?" Cash practically purred.

Double ouch. But also, yes, she was. She ignored him and headed for the seat across from Jesse—until he said, "I didn't call you worse... Maybe once in the heat of the moment, I might have said something I wish I could take back. Cash is an asshole."

Her throat seized at his words, and she bit back the stupid desire to ask what the hell he'd called her. Or thought of her. Deep down, she already knew.

"I can hear you," Cash called from his seat.

"Well, I didn't lower my voice." Jesse might be speaking to him, but he kept his gaze on Hailey.

And she felt trapped, that inexplicable need to *run* taking over. She'd always been like this and hated it. But she couldn't seem to outrun—pun intended—the urge to flee whenever things got rough. Avoiding tough situations was her super-power—or the opposite of a superpower. Whatever. "Okay, well..." She paused, deciding not to sit across from him after all. There was a bed in the back area, so maybe she'd just go lie down and ignore the outside world for a moment. "I've got a headache, so—"

The world tilted on its axis as they hit a burst of turbulence. Vaguely she heard the pilot coming over the speakers, telling them they needed to buckle in, but she jerked forward, unable to stop herself from falling.

Jesse moved like lightning, catching her when she would have collided with him. But instead of setting her on her feet or settling her in the seat next to him, he tugged her onto his lap.

She wasn't sure what the hell she was thinking—okay, she wasn't thinking, at least not with her brain—but as he pulled her close, she straddled him.

As if it was the most natural thing in the world, as if she'd done it a hundred times. Well, she had, once upon a time. And a lot more than a hundred. They'd been rabid for each other, obsessed and possessive. Two teens who'd never had anything of their own, not really, and then they'd found each other.

But they were adults now, and even if she wanted to deny it, wanted to erase their history, she couldn't erase the attraction burning between them. Not when it was so incendiary.

"Jesse—" She wasn't sure what she was going to say because he crushed his mouth to hers.

And heaven help her, she kissed him back, as longing welled up inside her, stole her breath. He tasted so familiar, and yet there was a difference now as he kissed her.

Consumed her.

Destroyed her without even realizing it.

She'd been so strong for years, locking up her emotions, ignoring all her needs, but everything came bubbling up to the surface as he teased his tongue against hers, as he gripped the back of her head in a tight, dominating hold.

Suddenly they were moving, and she thought the worst, but realized it wasn't turbulence now. Jesse had stood, was carrying her...to the back room.

The bedroom. She tore her mouth back, stared at him. "We can't—"

"We can do whatever the hell we want." He sounded like a man possessed as he slammed the door shut behind them.

And who was she kidding? She wasn't stopping this inevitable train wreck. If this was the only time she got him, because *clearly* he'd lost all his senses, she was going to take what he offered in the here and now.

She grabbed at his shirt, shoved it up and over his head, hating the brief gap in time where his lips weren't on hers. Because his taste was everything she remembered, had obsessed about for years. How was it possible that he was even better than her memories?

"I'm not going to be gentle," he growled against her mouth, even as they fell onto the bed.

"Don't care," she managed to rasp out. She didn't want gentle—didn't deserve it. She knew she'd hurt him years ago, even if it had been for the right reasons.

He shoved at her pants, managed to get them off, along with her panties. Then he murmured something against her mouth—she wasn't sure what—as he cupped her mound.

As he did, he shuddered against her. He hadn't even attempted to penetrate her, was simply holding on to her sex as he bit her bottom lip. "I want to go down on you." His words barely sounded human at this point. "But I want inside you more."

"I want you inside me too." Reaching between their bodies, she got the button of his pants free, and thankfully he took over, stripping quickly before he loomed over her.

Hard, built, powerful. And his cock was as beautiful as she remembered, jutting out obscenely as he crawled over her.

She belatedly realized that she still had her sweater on, but he shoved it up over her breasts before he captured one nipple through her bra. Didn't even bother to tug it down, simply sucked through the sheer material, making her buck against him.

She grasped onto his erection as he teased her nipples, flicking and gently biting as heat flooded through her.

She'd been touch-starved for so long that she felt as if she might come just from this alone. Breathing erratically, she stroked his hard length, tried to focus, but rolled her hips upward as he sucked her nipple again. She was searching for something—for him.

Her body needed him, and only him, inside her. "Jesse," she rasped out, not sure what she wanted to say. How about that she'd never gotten over him? She'd tried to lock down thoughts of him for years, but it was useless.

He cupped her mound again, and this time he slid a finger inside her, groaned as he felt how slick she was. "You're so wet."

No one had ever turned her on like he did. Ever. And ooooh, he slid another finger inside her. Started thrusting in and out in a steady rhythm.

She could barely think as he stroked inside her, knew she was close to coming. Hell, she'd been close to climax since he'd gotten her clothes off. Holding on to his erection, she guided him to her entrance even as he withdrew his fingers. "I'm on the pill," she rasped out since he hadn't brought up condoms.

"I don't care." His words came out a rumble, that possessive boy she'd known now a man on the razor's edge of losing control.

And she didn't care either. Didn't care about anything but this moment with him.

Slowly, almost too slowly, he slid inside her, his thickness filling her inch by inch. Her head rolled back from the pleasure of him stretching her, but he captured her mouth with his, refusing to let her get away from him.

His kisses were demanding, hungry, as he began thrusting inside her. And she nearly went off just from the feel of him, but when he reached between their bodies, rubbed her clit, she lost her tiny battle for control.

Because control didn't exist between them.

Her climax wasn't a slow build. It was a wrecking ball, slamming into her, pleasure punching out to all her nerve endings as he continued thrusting. She knew she cried out, couldn't have held back if she'd tried.

Which she didn't, because screw it.

He growled something she couldn't make out as his thrusts grew more intense, and then he was climaxing alongside her—inside her.

Time stopped as they both found their release. Only the two of them existed in the bubble of pleasure as he buried his face against her neck, bit down, marking her for everyone to see in a totally primal way that should have repelled her but did the exact opposite. The little bite of pain made her jerk against him and unexpectedly prolonged her orgasm, sending another wave of heat curling through her.

Finally, he collapsed on top of her, his expression dark and intense instead of relaxed as he looked down at her, as he cupped one breast possessively. "Was I too rough?" His question was unexpected.

She shook her head, fought the stupid wave of emotion that threatened to drown her in its wake. She wanted to tell him that it had been perfect, magical, absolute heaven. All she got out was a raspy, "No."

Still watching her closely, he tugged her sweater all the way over her head now, tossed it to the side. Then he grabbed his own sweater and pulled it over her head. "We'll be landing soon," he murmured. "And you're wearing my sweater."

She...so did not know what to say to that. Didn't know what to say to any of this. And she really didn't know what to do when he grabbed a washcloth from the attached bathroom and cleaned between her legs so sweetly and reverently. So she simply savored the feel of him being so gentle with her, knowing that it would never last.

Almost on cue, right as Jesse finished, the pilot came over the speaker, announcing their impending descent, and, oh wow, was she glad for it. Even if she knew she'd have to face Cash out in the main cabin in a moment. *Whatever.* Better than having to talk to Jesse about any of this.

Pretty much beyond words, she grabbed her pants and tugged them on when she couldn't find her panties. And she was too embarrassed to ask Jesse to help her look when he was watching her so closely. As if he thought she might break apart or something.

Ducking her head to avoid his gaze, she hurried out from the cabin and paused by her seat, grabbed her socks and shoes she'd discarded earlier.

Cash just looked at her, eyebrows raised.

"Shut up," she muttered, no heat in her voice, before she went to the front of the plane and strapped in.

To her surprise, Jesse sat right next to her a few moments later. "This isn't over between us," he finally said, low enough for only her to hear.

"I didn't think it was." *Liar.* She'd totally thought that was a one-time thing. She paused as she contemplated her next words. "I couldn't find my panties," she finally whispered. "We need to get them before we disembark." She didn't mind going commando but didn't relish the thought of his pilot or cleaning crew finding her undergarments. It was just weird.

"I've got them." The look he gave her was dark and sensual and ooooh...

It took a moment before she realized that he meant he was keeping them. Snapping her mouth shut, she looked straight ahead, trying to make sense of any of this.

And failing.

CHAPTER 10

Eight years ago

Hailey,

The news has been bad recently in your area (if you're still there), and not that I expect a response at this point, but I hope you're staying safe. We're all worried about you. And if you ever want to reach out, we're still here. I'm still here, as your friend or more. But always as your friend, no matter what. I hope you enjoy the care package. (Easton picked out the Christmas tree and was very proud of himself for it.)

—Jesse

***

Hey assface,

Is it cool that I still call you that? I won't hold my breath waiting for a response. ;) So school sucks, and even with a scholarship, I hate it. I know I sound whiny, but I don't care. I'm not even taking the kind of classes that Jesse and Easton are, and I still hate it. Easton is buried in school and excelling (shocker to exactly no one). Jesse is buried in whatever he's been doing lately. His last app took off, and I'm congratulating myself on investing in it.

Other than school, I've been trying to date. That's the only part of college I actually like. But then I see what's going on where you are (are you still there?), and everything just feels like a waste of time. I don't know what's wrong with me, and since I don't even know if you'll get these or respond, it's kind of easier to be open. I can't tell Jesse or Easton any of this because they have their own shit to deal with.

Oooh, Easton dated this guy from one of his classes, but it didn't work out. Now they're friends at least with no lingering awkwardness. They're both super nerds, and I really like the guy, but Easton needs someone to take charge, not someone exactly like him.

I talked to an army recruiter. Still not sure what I want to do with my life, but it's good to have options. Makes me feel less caged in.

I hope you're staying safe. We all miss you.

—Cash

***

Hailey,

Winter break just started, and I'm already dreading the time off from school. For Christmas Eve, I'll be hanging out with some friends from my program, and then on Christmas the three of us will be getting together. No one is cooking, though

Cash said he might try his hand at a turkey. I voted to get takeout as I don't relish the idea of calling the Fire Department if he sets something on fire.

Something is going on with Cash, even though he doesn't talk about it. It's like there's a darkness in him. Or maybe that's the wrong word. But he's restless, and I don't expect him to finish out the year. Which is a shame as he's so bright. But we all have to make our own choices.

Jesse is wrapped up in something new he won't tell any of us about. No real details anyway. Is it okay that I talk about him? I don't want to step over your boundaries, and I'm not sure what you want to know at this point. We all miss you—that's something that's never changed. Oh, the Christmas tree is from me, don't let Cash tell you otherwise. He had the audacity to say he was going to claim it was his idea. It was *not*.

I'm always here if you want to talk.

Sincerely,

Easton

CHAPTER 11

—We're all just one choice away from a different life.—

Jesse moved out in front of Hailey as they descended the jet, and he knew without looking that Cash had her booked in from behind. It didn't matter that she was one of the most capable people he knew, she was his to protect.

Always had been.

And Cash viewed her like a sister, would kill to protect her too. Though she'd hate for them to even think that.

Not that he cared at this point. After what had just happened between them, something dark and primal inside him had flared to life. Though who was he kidding? It had just been dormant. Wasn't like his obsession with her had ever gone away; he'd simply managed to contain it.

An SUV was waiting for them, just as he'd set up, in this quiet private airport in the middle of nowhere Kentucky.

"Just be on standby," he said to his longtime pilot, Jack Cooper. A handsome bastard. Why had he never noticed how good-looking the guy was? Jesse frowned, which made Jack frown in turn.

"Of course, sir. Is everything okay?" Jack pushed his sunglasses back on his head, his expression thoughtful and concerned. "I've already put your duffel bags in the back of the SUV."

Ah, as if that was what he'd been worried about. "Yes, everything is fine. Thank you." What was he going to say? Stop being so good-looking? Don't look at Hailey? Come to think of it, he could absolutely say the second thing. But he resisted the urge to go full-on caveman. At least right now. He reserved the right to do it later. He'd just marked Hailey in the back cabin, and she was wearing his mark on her neck and his actual sweater, so he could calm the hell down.

"Come on," Cash demanded, sliding into the front passenger seat.

Jesse waved off the driver and opened the back door for Hailey, who gave him a curious look. But she slid into the middle row, and he moved in right behind her so that their legs were touching.

In the front, Cash messed around with the radio as the driver silently steered them toward the exit.

Hailey nudged him once, then whispered, "I want my panties back."

He shook his head even as he shoved his hand in the pocket opposite her, fingered the scrap of lace—and wished he was fingering something else. "Mine now."

"I'm just going to say this once, in case the two of you need a reminder—the front isn't soundproofed. There's not even a partition." Cash's tone was dry, if amused.

"Oh, shut up, Cash," they both said, practically in unison.

Because apparently some things hadn't changed.

Hailey shot Jesse a slightly amused look, then seemed to catch herself and looked away. Oh no, his kitten wasn't getting away from him. Never again.

"You have the address?" Jesse said to the driver.

"Yes, sir."

The man nodded, then fell silent again, which Jesse was thankful for. He'd reached out to his private security company for someone to drive them around with no questions asked. He didn't know this man, but Jesse had worked with the company a long time and trusted their discretion.

Cash kept messing with the radio, then started singing to himself—loudly.

"Jesus, Cash, you sound like a drunk cat." Hailey mock covered her ears. "Give us all a reprieve."

"Only if you tell me more about Reese and why I'm not her type." He turned in his seat, his expression pure, charming Cash.

"Wait, is that why you're singing so terribly? To demand information?" Hailey stared at him in horror.

"No, he actually thinks he can sing," Jesse murmured as he responded to an email on his phone.

"I *can* sing. You two just have terrible taste." He sniffed imperiously, then glanced at their driver. "What do you think?"

"That you won't be winning any karaoke nights, sir." Their driver was an older man with salt-and-pepper hair, and his tone was bone dry.

His response made Hailey laugh, and Jesse devoured that sound, the joy rolling off her. "Aww, man, that's such a polite way of telling you that you suck donkey balls," she said, still laughing next to him.

He found himself smiling as she continued laughing. He'd missed her laugh more than he realized.

Cash frowned at her, opened his mouth, and Jesse swore he could see something smart-ass about to fly out. "Don't even go there," he snapped.

Which of course made Cash grin. "Fine, but tell me about Reese. I need something to keep my mind off...everything."

Hailey's expression shifted, and Jesse knew she was thinking about Easton. He was too, and hadn't stopped since his friend had been taken. They'd still received no ransom demand—and at this point Jesse wasn't expecting one.

This was about something else. He just hoped that whatever it was, it kept Easton alive.

"I don't know what you want to know. Reese is funny and smart and...I'm pretty sure she'd eat you alive. Plus you're rich, so that's a strike against you."

He blinked in surprise, but didn't push. Instead, he turned away from them and got very, very silent.

"Look, that's not a bad thing, Cash. I mean...you're great, and I love you, and I'm sure you have no problem with the ladies—"

"Oh, please stooooop." Cash still didn't turn around at all, and Jesse couldn't read his tone.

Not that Jesse was too concerned about the other man. But he sure as shit didn't like hearing Hailey say she loved him, even if it was platonic.

Sighing, Hailey looked at her phone. "We're only ten minutes out from the first place," she said to Jesse, then a little quieter. "Is this guy discreet?"

"I see nothing and say nothing," the man answered from the front. "I was hired to escort you and keep to myself. Obviously I will not partake in robbing a bank, for example, but I'm a silent shadow here to help you."

Hailey grinned up at Jesse. "I'm going to try to poach him."

Jesse didn't respond, couldn't. Not when she was smiling at him like that, so open and free, for just a fraction in time.

Then she looked away at an incoming alert on her phone. She held it out so he could read the text from Reese.

It was a bunch of pictures of an empty office building and a message that read: *Place is deserted for the most part other than the lobby. There are cameras everywhere, but I hacked in and disabled them. They might have caught us coming into the parking lot, but we wore masks.*

"Glad we brought balaclavas now," he murmured before handing the phone to Cash to read.

"Have you heard anything from the Feds?" Hailey asked when Cash handed her the phone back.

Jesse shook his head. "No, and I don't expect to. They took over because I pushed, but I don't think they'll give us regular updates."

Sighing, she sat back against the seat and to his surprise leaned slightly into him. He wasn't sure if she even realized, but he leaned into her as well.

Things had shifted between them—and he wasn't letting her go.

CHAPTER 12

—Good things never last.—

"If you try to tell me I need to stay behind, I'll punch you both in the junk." Hailey tucked her braid under her wig before pulling on a mask. Her fake blonde hair would be sticking out underneath for any potential security cameras. "Because this is literally what I do for a living."

"You break into places for a living?" Cash eyed her with curiosity as he tugged his own balaclava on.

After driving by a warehouse with a huge, empty parking lot, their driver, Wilson, had parked about half a mile from the place, pulling off the two-lane highway into the woods. Unlike the site that Reese and Elijah had checked out, this facility was in a rural part of Kentucky.

The nearest home was six miles away, and the warehouse wasn't in a city or town, but was part of the county. Which should make things easier for them for multiple reasons. She'd checked out the sheriff's department, and they had only two guys working right now for the entire county. So even if they set off an alarm, they'd have time before someone responded to the call. They also didn't have to worry about any nosy neighbors or businesses.

"I mean, I don't exclusively break into places or anything, but sometimes it's part of my job." She had her tablet in hand, held it out for Jesse and Cash. "This is where the cops are now so we have a great window of time to act. But I should be asking if you two want to do this? You're the ones with more to lose if we get caught."

Jesse's jaw clenched, and he actually glared at her as he tugged his balaclava on.

"I wasn't saying that you care less for Easton or anything, just that—" She shut her mouth when even Cash glared at her. "I'm sorry. I'm a jackass."

"You're not a jackass," Jesse murmured as he grabbed the drone case, then shut the back of the SUV. "But understand that neither of us care about our money or reputation compared to how much we love Easton."

"I know that." And she hadn't meant to insinuate otherwise. She cleared her throat, trying to move past her stupid mouth. Their driver was in the front seat, on his phone, completely ignoring the three of them, which worked well for Hailey. "Okay, so we get in, take some pictures, see what this place really is, then get out. And if we see anyone, we run. This is just about information gathering at this point. I'm hoping we'll find something useful, but considering that Reese and Elijah found a whole lot of nothing, I'm not holding my breath."

Both men nodded, standing at alert. *Okay, then.* She was used to working with her Redemption Harbor Security team, and they were all former military—though Cash was actually former army, and Jesse had learned self-defense from a former Spec Ops guy on his security, so she knew they could both handle themselves.

Ask her how she knew that little tidbit about Jesse's training. Oh right, a little bit of sneaky stalking.

"I'm going to take point," she started.

"Ah, how about I take point?" Cash said, interrupting. "You're the one with the drone-flying skills and the hacking skills."

"You guys can't fly a drone?" She looked between the two of them disbelievingly, especially since she knew for a fact that Jesse was backing a new prototype of drone that would probably make him another couple million once it hit the market.

Jesse cleared his throat, looking slightly abashed.

"That's what I thought. Jesse, you fly the drone. And fine, you can take point, Cash. You have more on-the-ground experience than me anyway."

Wordlessly, they made their way through the woods, using makeshift walking paths—probably from hunters—to get close to the border of the warehouse's property. It was a gray day, their breath curling in front of them as they trekked over the brittle grass.

"All right, this is close enough." Jesse spoke quietly as they neared the property line.

Through the trees they could see the parking lot and building, but as far as she could tell there weren't any signs of life—no cars, no security, nothing. Not that the lack of all that necessarily meant anything. There could be people inside.

She and Cash were quiet as Jesse got to work, quickly deploying the drone with an efficiency that she could admit was impressive. She'd logged a lot of hours because of her job—in the Marines and the one she had now—and he guided the machine even better than she did.

As he steered the drone high above the warehouse, she made notes of each security camera location. "They don't seem to be motion activated at least," she murmured.

"No, these are fairly shitty actually. I mean, not the bottom of the barrel, but no real pharma company is going to use this kind of equipment, especially not Innovative Labs."

Jesse frowned as he moved around, looking for a good way to infiltrate the drone.

"There," he finally said. "If we move in from this angle, only one camera might catch us. And we'll have enough time to get inside and look around."

After he packed up the drone and propped the case against one of the nearby oak trees, they hurried through the woods until they were southwest of the structure.

"Everyone ready?" Cash looked at the two of them, and when they nodded, he said, "We're silent now. No one speaks in case there's any sort of recording devices inside."

She looked back at Jesse, nodded once, then followed after Cash, the three of them sprinting for one of the back doors. She turned up the volume on the handheld radio she'd attached to the back of her pants so they could hear the chatter of the local deputies. This was old-school but worked in a rural place.

Even though Cash was taking point, she moved in front of the door and quickly picked the lock—and again, it wasn't top-of-the-line with biometrics. Which was just plain odd for what this place was supposed to be.

Cash moved in front of her, and she was very aware of Jesse's presence behind her as they stepped into the building.

Cash flipped on the nearest switch and...a flicker of overhead lights came on. She turned on the rest of them, and more lights sputtered on in a ripple, one after the other, illuminating... *nothing*. An empty building.

She looked up at the two men, and Jesse nodded once before they fanned out. She sprinted across the floor, her sneakers making squeaking sounds as she headed for a door on the other side. To her surprise, Jesse was right next to her, a weapon held loosely in his gloved hand.

She frowned at the sight of it since they'd agreed to no weapons—though she did have pepper spray, one of her favorite things ever—but didn't say a word. Once they reached the other door, she tested the handle, but Jesse moved her out of the way with his body before sweeping in, weapon out.

Oh yeah, he'd had more than just a little training because he held that thing like a pro. But once he saw the room was empty other than built-in metal shelving, they stepped back out into the main room and tried another door.

Ten minutes later she heard an alert on the radio about a silent alarm going off at their address, so she motioned to Jesse and Cash, and they hurried out, racing back the way they'd come.

Normally she liked to do more recon and to completely disable any security systems, but this was essentially on the fly. By the time they made it back to the SUV, she could hear a siren in the distance.

So they worked quickly, shucking their masks, her wig and changing into different sweaters before Wilson, their quiet driver, steered out of the hiding spot. And two minutes later, as they headed down the two-lane highway to the interstate, they drove by a police cruiser that didn't pause as it passed them.

Hailey shoved out a breath as their driver pulled onto the interstate.

"That was a whole lot of nothing," Cash grumbled.

"Maybe, maybe not," she murmured. "But I don't think we should waste time looking at the other addresses. Unless either of you do?"

"Your team already looked at two and found nothing," Jesse murmured. "I think you're right. We should head back home."

She liked the way he said *home*, had the sudden thought that she wished his home was hers. Shaken by the random thought, she simply nodded. Home wasn't with him, not anymore.

Though it had been at one point. Walls and a roof had never mattered to her, just his presence. Unable to meet his gaze for fear that he'd somehow read her mind, she pulled out her phone and texted her team as well as Skye, updating everyone on what they'd found.

She knew that Skye's crew was working on something big right now, but thankfully Gage was always willing to help with any type of research.

Unfortunately, she wasn't sure what the hell else to look for. "Would it be a total breach of whatever for you to let me look at Easton's work?" she suddenly asked, looking at Jesse. He'd already sent over all of Easton's work files, but she wanted to see his lab. "Like his office space itself? Maybe talk to some of the people he works with? I know the Feds have already, but... I'm less scary than an FBI agent."

Nodding, he looked at his phone. "We'll stop by as soon as we get back."

Well, that was easy. Unable to look at him for too long, she simply nodded her thanks, then leaned her head against the back of the seat. She shouldn't be thinking about what she'd done with Jesse only hours ago. Too bad the sounds and images—and sensations—were right at the forefront of her brain, just waiting for any downtime she had to wave all the memories in front of her like a giant flag.

To remind her of all the goodness she'd had before. And now that she'd had another brief taste, she knew it was a matter of time before she lost it again.

Lost Jesse.

Because there were things he didn't know, things she'd never been brave enough to tell him.

Sighing, and against her better judgment, she leaned into him, settling her head against his shoulder. To her surprise, he slid one big hand on her leg, gently set it against her knee. So she linked her arm through his and placed her hand over his.

He might not be hers anymore, but she could pretend he was for just a little bit.

CHAPTER 13

Henry Silva didn't like coming here, but there was nothing to be done about it. He'd had his men bring Easton Reed, certifiable genius, to one of his safe houses, drug him, and try to loosen him up.

Because this was the kind of individual he couldn't use brute force with, couldn't torture. Unfortunately. Not when he needed what was inside Easton's head. Soon he'd move him to a designated work space, but he needed Reed dependent on him, to want the drugs he was slowly pumping him full of.

One of his guards was outside the bedroom and simply nodded as he approached.

He stepped into the room, saw the genius lying on the mattress, staring up at the ceiling. And when Easton looked over at him, his eyes were glassy, unfocused.

He stepped back out into the hallway. "I thought you were pulling back on the doses." They'd overestimated the first couple, and the man had gotten sick.

"I did, but he's refusing to eat unless I force him. And you were very clear that we can't use force with him," the guard said quietly. The man was a former Ranger, dishonorably discharged, and seemed to get off on causing others pain. But he knew how to follow orders, so Reed wasn't truly being injured.

Maybe drugging him was the wrong move. Henry hadn't planned to take the man originally, but things had changed recently.

"That still stands. Dose him again to knock him out, then move him. I think we're handling this the wrong way." Something he hated to admit, but he hadn't gotten to where he was by not being able to pivot—despite what some people thought.

Easton Reed was a man used to his lab, a clean, pristine living space. Maybe if he put him in a work environment, gave him food and clothing, he'd be more compliant, even without drugs. Because the only flaw in his plan to drug Reed was that it could affect him neurologically. And he needed the man's brain.

Reed was a nerd at his core and lived and breathed science. Maybe he simply needed to be in a familiar environment.

Getting someone to do what you wanted always took finesse. For some, torture or even the threat of pain was enough. For others, blackmail was the best option. It caused fear, and people almost always acted in their best interests when they didn't want the world privy to their dirty little secrets.

And he had so much dirt on people—another reason he was where he was. Unfortunately, he hadn't been able to get anything on Reed. The man lived like a monk. He'd had his people start working on building a fake trail of money online to cast a dark shadow around Easton, but he needed what was in the man's head before he killed him.

Because knowledge was the ultimate power.

Henry simply had to play this right. Especially since the Feds were involved now. The local cops couldn't find their asses with both hands. But the FBI was a different story. And he wanted to know who the hell that woman who'd broken into Easton's place had been. He'd had one of his guys sitting on the man's apartment just in case, and he'd seen some random woman breaking in through the window. From the sixth floor. Unfortunately, he didn't even have a picture of her so he couldn't run her ID.

Then his guy had gone and gotten himself arrested by the Feds. At least the idiot wasn't talking anyway.

As Henry headed out of the safe house, he frowned at an incoming text, then froze for a moment before getting into his car. He'd parked in the garage so no one would see him. Before leaving, he read the incoming texts again, digested everything.

Someone had broken into multiple warehouses owned by his business partner. The places were empty so it wasn't as if the individuals breaking in had taken anything. It was the fact that three separate places had been broken into all around the same time.

A targeted effort.

They used the places as fronts, usually to funnel R&D money into their own pockets, but no one should know anything about them. Not when they went to great lengths to keep their business private. He definitely had to, considering his job.

If he was being investigated by the FBI, he should have heard something about it by now, especially considering the man who worked for him.

His fixer.

Annoyed now, he angrily called the man who solved all his problems so he didn't have to get his hands dirty. "I think we have an issue."

CHAPTER 14

—Whoever said whatever doesn't kill you makes you stronger was a moron. Lots of stuff that doesn't kill you makes you weaker; gunshot wounds for instance.—

Hailey worked on her laptop as Jesse drove through the throng of traffic. At three o'clock, the number of vehicles on the road seemed excessive, but she figured this was just what the DC/Virginia area was like. It was just the two of them now, having gone separate ways with Cash once they'd landed back in Virginia.

And maybe it was just her, but things between them felt...awkward. But she didn't think it was just her.

"So what are you going to do with my panties anyway?" she asked into the quiet.

He jerked slightly, but the wheel barely moved under his expert grip. "Put them under my pillow tonight. Maybe the panty fairy will bring me something amazing."

She stared at his stoic profile before a burst of laughter escaped. "The panty fairy, that's a new one." Smiling to herself, she went back to her screen. But then she paused, looked back up at him. "You get visits from the panty fairy a lot?"

"This will be the first time."

She sniffed once before she looked back at her screen.

Then he surprised her. "So I probably should have asked before—not that the answer would have mattered, if I'm being honest—but I take it you're not dating anyone."

"I don't date. And I'm on the pill because of...the same issues I had years ago." But now she was wondering if he was dating anyone. If he was, Easton had never mentioned it during one of their talks. She gritted her teeth, forcing herself to not ask the thing she wanted to ask. Because she had self-control. Normally. "Are you dating anyone?" So much for self-control.

He simply grunted in response.

What the hell did that mean? She didn't have the courage to push because she didn't want to know about his dating habits. Ugh, the thought was just... She couldn't even put it into words. See, this was exactly why she'd tried to avoid thinking of him over the years.

And had only stalked him a little bit from time to time.

"Wait a minute..." Her fingers flew across the keyboard as that familiar buzz hit.

"What is it?"

"I'm not sure just yet. But I think I might have something." Oh please let her have a lead. "Whoever set up that fake account in an LLC under Easton's name made a mistake. Or I think they did..."

Thankfully he was silent as she continued to work.

"Okay, so it looks like all of the LLCs for the fake companies we visited were set up by various people, who might not even be real. They're performing transactions with other LLCs offshore, and then these offshore companies are lending money or investing in various businesses."

"It's a loan-back scheme," he murmured.

"Yes, something I honestly don't fully understand. But what I do understand is that one of these offshore companies is one that funded Easton's fake account originally. And..."

She utilized a program that Gage Yates had created to search county records all over the country.

"The attorney of record on most of these is the same, Ian Warren. He hasn't inherently done anything wrong other than set up accounts for his clients. But he's got to be involved in whatever this shit is." Hailey wasn't sure what was going on yet, but the fact that the LLCs they'd visited had been set up by this same attorney who'd set up an LLC that had eventually funded Easton's account was too much to ignore.

"He's a shark. Tried to pull me in as a client years ago, but I politely declined. Most of his clients are in politics. And it's a select few. Not my crowd."

"That might narrow things down, then."

"Yeah," Jesse murmured, frowning, but she could see the wheels in that big brain of his turning. "We're here." He nodded as they pulled up to the security gate.

Blinking, she looked up and half smiled at the security guy as Jesse rolled down his window.

"Hey Roland, how's it going?" Jesse's voice was cordial, and she wasn't at all surprised that he knew the first name of the security guy here. He had a way with names and faces that had always impressed her. And he was good with people—or at least not terrible like she was. She preferred her computer, books, and hiking to most people.

"Can't complain. I'm really sorry about Easton. Everyone here is hoping he's found soon."

"Thank you. We are too," he said, motioning to Hailey, who simply nodded at the man. "Roland, this is Hailey, a childhood friend of Easton's."

Roland gave her a sympathetic look before he focused on Jesse again.

"Anyone here right now?" Jesse continued.

"Other than security, everyone else cleared out twenty minutes ago."

Made sense considering it was just after normal business hours and getting dark.

"I won't be here long, but I appreciate everything you do here. Thanks for holding down the fort."

The man smiled at Jesse once and tipped an imaginary hat before he waved them through the gates.

"Do you stop by here a lot?"

"Only to check on Easton, make sure he's taking care of himself." There was a hint of something in his voice she couldn't quite define.

On impulse she reached out and squeezed his arm. "We're going to find him."

"That's what I keep telling myself. I just... I worry about him. And I know he's a grown-ass man. A very smart man. An actual *genius*. I just..."

"He's the baby, even if it's only by one year," she said quietly. "We'll always worry about him."

"Did you worry about him when you were gone?"

She noticed he'd simply said gone and not "when you abandoned all of us." And for some reason, that was even worse. The careful way he'd phrased it.

Clearing her throat, she said, "I worried about the three of you every second of every day. And even though I never mailed them, I wrote you guys letters," she rasped out as he pulled into a parking spot right at the front. Before he could respond, she jumped from the vehicle and dashed away the stupid tears that wanted to have a party on her face.

Once she got herself under control, she met Jesse on the sidewalk by the front of his vehicle—and totally avoided making eye contact.

Thankfully he wasn't in the mood to push her because all he said was, "This way."

She fell in step beside him as they headed through the shiny glass doors of the main entrance and wasn't surprised at all to be greeted by more security here.

Two people, a man and a woman. And they looked a lot more serious than the man at the security gate. Roland had looked like the kind of guy you'd have a beer with at a local pub. These two had definitely been in the military, though which branch, or branches, she couldn't guess.

They were middle-aged as well, but they were all sharp edges and no smiles. The woman's dark hair was pulled back into a neat braid, and the man's blond hair was cut high and tight.

And Jesse didn't smile at them or shoot the shit. Simply said, "We're headed up," with no explanations or introductions.

Clearly professionals, the two nodded right back and retained their posts.

"You should have one of them at the front gate," Hailey murmured once they were in the elevators. She figured someone was watching them on the security feed, but whatever.

Jesse just grinned. "Roland is a former Ranger and always armed. He was only friendly because he likes me and I was with a beautiful woman. His nickname is 'Mr. Hardass' around here."

She blinked in surprise (and tried not to bask in the beautiful comment too much). "Seriously?"

"Yep. If someone forgets their badge, he doesn't care if he knows them or has hung out with them outside of work. He sends them home to find it, no exceptions."

"That's what I get for judging a book by the cover. He seems so nice and friendly, and I was just thinking he'd be the kind of guy you'd like to get a beer with. Not you specifically, but like a general you."

Jesse laughed softly. "I hear you. And I think in his off time he is an incredibly nice guy. He's got three girls, all in high school, is married to his high school sweetheart, and by all accounts, dotes on all of them. But he takes his job very seriously."

"I like hearing you laugh." The words were out before she could censor them, before she could tell her big, dumb mouth to zip it.

He sucked in a breath, and when he turned to look at her, his eyes were flinty, but not from anger. Something a whole lot different. "You make it impossible to hate you. Even when you left, I could never hate you."

Before she could digest his words, even process them, he had her pinned up against the elevator wall, his mouth crushed to hers in a brutal claiming. And that was exactly what it was.

She dug her fingers into his shoulders as she kissed him back, but before she could lean into it, the elevator dinged, and he stepped back.

Blinking, she was unsteady on her feet as they stepped off the metal box of death and onto shiny white floors.

The brightness helped her get her equilibrium back a lot faster than anything else could have after that...whatever that had been, because it was more than a kiss. Down the hallway in front of them were what appeared to be labs and probably testing-type rooms. Probably still called labs too—science was not her thing.

"His office is around here?" she murmured as she fell in step with Jesse again. The rooms all had huge glass windows framing them so there was no privacy in any of these spaces. Which was probably the point.

"No, his office is a floor down, but his lab is at the end of this—"

A rumble started under her feet, and she froze. *What the hell?*

Before she could move, Jesse shoved her back and tackled her to the ground—as a wave of heat and thunder washed over them.

She screamed, the sound drowned out under the explosion as Jesse covered her body with his. She wrapped her arms around him, trying to protect him as rubble and plaster rained down on them.

She wasn't sure how long they lay like that, but she eventually became aware of a ringing in her ears and water cascading over them. It took her a moment to realize that Jesse was talking to her and that the water was the sprinkler system.

"What?" Was she shouting?

"Can you sit up?"

She nodded because she could read his lips. As she sat up with him, she stared in horror at the devastation in front of them.

The end of the hallway was gone, the entire floor caved in below. The ceiling had been ripped away as well, and there was so much glass everywhere, the tempered pieces scattered like a million stars over what was left of the hallway.

The lights flickered on and off, and multiple alarms sounded as water showered down on the hallway, the labs, and the missing floor.

Blinking, she realized Jesse was saying something as he stood, stumbled once. She shoved up, momentarily disoriented from the sudden movement, but managed to steady herself.

Wrapping her arm around his middle, she turned and pointed toward the other end of the hallway from where they'd come. She ignored the water that splashed them as they started to move.

"... the stairs." Jesse's voice was suddenly crystal clear as her ears popped.

The alarm sounded a thousand times louder, blaring through the building now that she could hear.

She looked up at him. "Are you okay?" she shouted over the noise.

"I'm fine." But he didn't look fine. And she didn't blame him. Because what had just happened? "But we need to get the hell out of here in case there's another bomb."

"Bomb?" Of course it had been a bomb. What was wrong with her? Had the blast scrambled her brain? She'd witnessed more than her share of IED damage in Afghanistan.

"This wasn't an accident. We have too many precautions in place, sensors, alarms..." He swore softly as they reached the stairs, and she could see him blaming himself for something that clearly wasn't his fault.

"Whatever this was, it's not on you, Jesse. And—" Frowning when she saw blood on the side of his neck, she stepped back from him, gently took his upper arms, and turned him away from her. "Shit, you've got shrapnel in your back."

"I'm fine." He shoved the door open with a clang.

But he wasn't fine at all. And she didn't think she was either.

CHAPTER 15

—It's fine. I'm fine. Everything is fine.—

Hailey leaned against the back of the open ambulance, hands shoved into the pockets of the scrubs someone had given her as the EMT finished looking over Jesse.

He'd been hit with what was essentially shrapnel from the explosion. Bits of glass and sheetrock and whatever else, and since his stubborn ass refused to go to the hospital, they were doing a thorough checkup right out here in the parking lot.

The Feds, fire department, a handful of cop cars, and multiple ambulances had taken over the parking lot and building. The firefighters were currently searching the building, looking for signs of life. There wasn't supposed to be anyone on that floor, and she really hoped that was true. Thankfully, the security team from the first floor was fine.

"Ms. West," Special Agent Parker approached the ambulance, his expression tight. "I'd like to take your statement now if you're feeling up to it."

"Of course." She pushed off the vehicle, glad for the bite of wind in the air even if it was chilly with her still damp hair. The sprinklers had certainly done their job, dousing everything. The bit of pain grounded her better than anything else when she kept replaying that explosion in her mind, the way Jesse had thrown himself on top of her.

Right now he could be a hell of a lot more injured than the nicks and cuts from the flying glass. He could be...

She swallowed hard as she tried to banish the thought. The images that wanted to take over. It was hard though.

"She's not going anywhere without me," Jesse practically snarled, glaring daggers at the agent while the EMT finished putting on another bandage.

Her own arms had a few bandages from some light nicks, but thankfully they'd been out of the main area of the blast zone. "It's fine, Jesse."

"I'm good," he said to the EMT before tugging on a T-shirt he'd grabbed from his SUV earlier. He had a go-bag in his vehicle, and she desperately wished she'd had hers with her.

Sighing, the agent nodded at Jesse as he approached. "I can take statements from both of you. I've talked to security, and we're going to be combing over the security feeds, but I want to hear from both of you what happened." He gave Jesse a hard look. "It should be separately, but at this point I'm not bothering."

"I don't know what we can share that will help. We were walking down the hallway when everything exploded." She'd started to wrap her arms around herself when Jesse moved in close to her, slid an arm around her shoulders. "It all happened so fast, and we were lucky..." She shuddered.

Soaking up his presence, Hailey dropped her arms and wrapped one around Jesse, held him close.

"Why were you here in the first place?"

Oh, maybe she shouldn't answer. Thankfully Jesse spoke before she could. "I was taking Hailey to look at Easton's office. Where are you on the investigation?"

The man's jaw ticked once, but his expression was otherwise neutral. "As I've explained before, I can't talk about an ongoing investigation. And why were you going to his office?"

"I've hired Ms. West and Redemption Harbor Security to look into Easton's kidnapping, something you already know."

"I'm not interfering in your investigation," Hailey added when the man cut her a hard look. "Just looking for different angles. And if I get any solid intel, I'll pass it along. Unfortunately, everything exploded before I got a chance to check things out."

"We already went over Mr. Reed's office with a fine-tooth comb."

"I'm sure you did, but I grew up with Easton and thought a fresh set of eyes in a place he spent a lot of time would help."

A slight shout caused all of them to turn, and to Hailey's surprise Special Agent Hazel Blake was striding their way. In a black jacket, black pants and low-heeled boots, she looked as she always did: no-nonsense and gorgeous. Relief flooded her to see a woman she knew fairly well on-site. If she had to guess, Hailey thought that maybe Skye had reached out to Hazel since they had a long history.

"Hey Parker, you wrapped up here?" Hazel asked, not bothering with small talk. Which, yeah, was about right.

The woman had been an Air Force Cobra pilot years ago and served with Leighton Cannon, one of the founders of Redemption Harbor Consulting.

"Almost. What are you doing here? I thought you were out of state." Parker frowned at Hazel.

"Just got back this morning, wrapped up the job. Harvey's on vacation." Her normal partner. "Since I'm flying solo and was in the area, the director asked me to stop by, see if you needed any help. The fire chief said he might have something, wants to talk to the agent in charge. I can finish taking statements if you need?"

He nodded at her, then looked back at Jesse and Hailey. "You can give your statement to Special Agent Blake," he murmured before heading toward the fire chief.

"I want to hug you right now, but I'll resist the urge." Hazel's voice was neutral as she eyed Hailey. Her jet-black hair was pulled back into a ponytail, and she had on emerald earrings Hailey knew had been a gift from her wife. "Parker doesn't know we're friends. So are you okay? Why aren't you both at the hospital?"

"Ah, we're both fine. and I'm pretending we're hugging right now," Hailey said, smiling. "Special Agent Hazel Blake, this is Jesse Lennox."

"Just call me Hazel, and you didn't answer my question. Skye's pissed, wants to know what's going on. Said you texted there was an explosion and it's been radio silence since."

Hailey frowned. "We don't need the hospital. I told her we were fine, and I'd check in once I wasn't surrounded by Feds."

"Yeah, well, she's a control freak, so I said I'd stop by."

"Your director didn't order you here?"

"Eh, I might have bent the facts a bit. He knows I'm here though because I offered to lend a hand." She glanced over her shoulder, eyed the handful of agents milling around. "Listen, what I'm about to say stays between us. Got it?" Now she looked at Jesse, her expression hard.

"Of course," he murmured, his arm still around Hailey's shoulders.

She liked it there.

"They found where your friend was being held before he was transported somewhere else."

"Wait, *what*? Easton was moved?"

"Yeah, that's what it looks like. His face was caught on a CCTV from a moving vehicle. It's brief, but it looks like he rolled down the window before someone grabbed him and rolled it back up."

"When did this happen?"

"About an hour ago. Give or take. From there, they traced the license of the vehicle back to the owner of an empty house. Place has been wiped clean for the most part, but they snagged some DNA from Easton Reed. He was there."

Shit. She'd probably gotten an alert on her laptop from the CCTV scans she had running, would look into the details as soon as possible. "So he's alive." *For now*, was all she could think, knew from the way Jesse straightened that he was thinking the same thing.

"Yeah. And I could lose my job for telling you, but I know you won't say anything."

"Never."

"Are you holding back anything about your friend? Anything shady he was into?" She looked between the two of them, her eyes searching.

Hailey looked up at Jesse, hoped he was on the same page when she looked back at Hazel. "He wasn't into anything, but someone went to a lot of trouble to make it look like he was funding terrorists. Someone set up a bank account in his name. Real sloppy work that anyone with two brain cells would be able to tell was set up on purpose. I shut down the fake account in his name though."

"Yeah, well, not before our people saw it," Hazel said.

"Hell," Jesse muttered.

"Do you have any idea who could have bombed your building?" Hazel asked, changing topics.

"No. I mean, none related to Easton. And honestly, *no*. I've got some competitors, but this is a side project for me. Something I'm doing because I have the money and believe in this. I'm not making money off this research, and I don't plan to in the future."

"I gathered that from the files we've got. And maybe that's the issue. Maybe someone blew this place up because they don't like that you might eventually be giving away medicine for free."

Jesse shook his head slowly. "Everything we have is backed up in the cloud..." He paused, looked down at Hailey. "Unless we've been compromised completely. I need to talk to my security, and I want you to look over our stuff as well."

"Of course," she said, nodding. So would Reese. "As soon as we get the hell out of here." To Hazel she said, "Are the Feds still looking for Easton even if they think he was funding terrorism?"

Hazel snorted softly. "Even harder now actually. We're going to find him, and if you discover something important and don't want to give it to Parker, pass it to me, and I can say I got it from an anonymous source. I'm pretty sure the director is going to officially put me on this case. I can make anything work, okay?"

"Can you finish taking our statement so we can get out of here?" Jesse asked, his phone up to his ear as he was clearly talking to someone in his security department.

"Yep." Hazel pulled out her tablet and began.

***

Jesse forced himself to stop pacing in his home office, knowing it was doing no one any good. Reese and Elijah were quietly working, and Hailey looked exhausted.

"So what did your people say?" Hailey leaned back in her chair, the circles under her eyes faint as she stretched her arms over her head.

They'd been back at his place for an hour after finally answering all the Feds' questions. While he'd been working with his team trying to figure out how someone had breached his business, Hailey had been looking at his online security.

"Same thing you did. Someone or multiple someones tried brute-force attacks on our security server, but so far nothing has been penetrated. They're beefing up security."

"Good. Your system is impressive..." She trailed off, looked back at her screen, then frowned. "Holy shit. Look at this, Jesse."

Something cracked in his chest at the casual way she said his name. He knew that absolutely nothing was settled between them, but he also knew he was never getting over her. There would be no closure with Hailey.

"What the hell?" He looked up at her mirrored screen on one of the wall monitors. "When was this?"

Jesse watched as David Beeker, one of his *own* security employees, walked into Easton's lab with a backpack, then walked back out a moment later, sans backpack. The screen glitched slightly, the pixels shifting before he blinked out of existence midstep down the hallway.

Hailey muttered a curse under her breath as she typed in a few more commands. "About an hour before you and I got there. And he almost covered his tracks, but not well enough. The Feds are going to strip this from the security feeds soon, if they haven't already. Do you know the guy?"

The man's picture popped up on-screen as she started to run a search for information on him.

"Name's Dave Beeker, he works for me, and I can have his address in moments. Come on," he said, already texting his head of security. He wasn't waiting for the Feds to confront Beeker.

Even as she stood, grabbed her laptop and backpack, she said, "Should we call the Feds on this one? They might even be talking to Beeker now."

"Not if we get there first," he growled. "I hired this guy and want to know what the hell is going on." And at the end of the day, he only trusted himself, Hailey, and her team to find Easton. He wouldn't just sit by and let someone else handle things.

"I'm still looking into Ian Warren," Reese said without looking up. "I've got him covered while you're gone. Just don't go dark without telling us."

"And watch each other's sixes," Elijah added, briefly looking up, nodding once at Jesse.

He blinked, but nodded.

"Should we bring one of your security guys?" Hailey asked.

"You think we can't handle this?"

She reached behind herself and patted her backpack. "No. I'm fully stocked with bear spray, a couple concussion grenades and a SIG, but backup is a good thing."

"I'm never letting you forget you just said that," Reese called out as they exited his office.

Hailey simply rolled her eyes. "Ignore her. I use backup. Aaaaall the time."

He was pretty sure she was lying, given her tone, but let that one go. "One of my guys will follow us. Also, you have *grenades*?" He wasn't sure what the hell to do with that info as they stepped into his four-car garage.

"Always be prepared." She gave a half salute. "That's one of my favorite mottos."

"So you carry a SIG in addition to the bear spray? Why didn't you use it yesterday morning?"

"Jesus, has it only been since yesterday?" she said as she slid into the passenger seat, exhaustion weaving through her words.

"Right?" Jesse was used to running on little sleep and tackling huge projects to the tune of forgetting everything else, but this was different.

A clock was ticking. Whoever had taken Easton wouldn't keep him alive forever. Whenever they got whatever the hell it was they wanted, Easton would cease to be useful.

"To answer your question—" she said as he zoomed out of the garage.

The exterior of his house and his gated property were lit up with security in mind, but it was after seven now, and darkness had taken over the city.

"I prefer bear spray or other nonlethal weapons if possible. I saw...well, I saw a lot of shit overseas. Even being in Intel, I got a front-row seat to the destructive power of man-made weapons. Don't get me wrong, I've used them, and I'm a proficient shot with my SIG. I just prefer nonlethal if possible. Much to the amusement of the rest of my team."

For some reason, he wasn't surprised. "How'd you transition back to civilian life? Was it difficult?" Jesse knew that Cash had struggled, though he'd tried to hide it. After his stint in the army, Cash had used all the investments he'd gotten returns on and started a small construction company—that had grown in leaps and bounds in the past four years and was now making billions. Everything the man touched turned to gold.

"Ah...yes and no. I don't know, maybe it's because I grew up bouncing around. It was easier to sort of frame it as moving on to another 'house' or chapter of my life, essentially. But also, working for Skye and Redemption Harbor Security has made things a lot easier. The rules of working with them are a lot different than if I'd gotten some corporate job. I know I'm making a difference, and I get to see the difference I'm making, the real people we help. So what about you? You've created some life-changing apps, including the one for military people transitioning back to civilian life."

"Did you use it?" He tried to sound casual, wasn't sure if he failed. He'd created it with her in mind.

"Oh yeah, it was amazing. And even better, it's super cheap," she added. "Jesse, that big brain of yours is really something else. I don't know how you come up with the ideas you do, but I and a lot of other people are incredibly grateful."

Something about her praise punched right through to the heart of him. He didn't know how to respond so remained silent as he took another left. One of his guys was following at a distance but understood not to interfere or follow them inside Beeker's condo building.

Rationally, he knew he should call the Feds, but he wasn't feeling rational right now. Hailey could have died in that explosion.

Her bright light could have been snuffed out in the blink of an eye and…Jesse couldn't imagine a world without her in it. Even when miles and an ocean had separated them, he'd known that she was still in the world, kicking ass and simply being her.

So screw Beeker and whatever his reasons were for what he'd done. Maybe Jesse'd call the Feds, but not until he got answers.

Because the man didn't get to almost kill Hailey and get away with it.

CHAPTER 16

—Sometimes an apology isn't enough.—

Hailey winced as Jesse slammed his fist against the condo's front door again. Squeezing his upper arm, she tugged him back. "He's not answering. Let's call the Feds." Never her first choice, but this guy had very likely planted a bomb, and he needed to be caught.

Jesse nodded. Then taking her off guard, he reared back and kicked the door open with one sharp thrust of his booted foot. The frame cracked, splintered under the impact.

Hoooooly shit.

"Jesse," she murmured, wincing again when she heard one of Beeker's neighbors open their door, then close it quickly. Well, they only had a few minutes at most before some type of law enforcement showed up.

Ignoring her, he stalked inside, rage rolling off him in almost palpable waves. The place was dark, and she'd quietly pulled out her bear spray when she heard a sort of moaning sound. *What the hell?*

She jerked to a stop next to Jesse when she spotted Beeker on a couch in his living room, curled in a ball and crying.

"I'm sorry," he sobbed as he looked up at Jesse from his couch, his chest heaving. "I saw the news. No one was supposed to be there! I'm so sorry." Another sob racked his body as he covered his face with a pillow.

"No one was killed," Hailey said loudly. "You made a mistake, but no one was hurt." Just slightly injured.

The red-faced man pulled the pillow down from his face and looked up at them, tears and snot all over his cheeks. *Gross.* He swiped at the mess. "No one was hurt? The news said they were digging for bodies."

"I don't care what the news said. No one was killed." Jesse's voice was razor-sharp, making Beeker flinch away from him as if he thought Jesse might strike him.

And considering the way Jesse looked right now, she wasn't so sure that he wouldn't.

Hailey stepped in front of him and sat on the coffee table. She kept her bear spray hidden but in her grasp. It didn't look like the guy had a weapon, but she wanted to be careful.

"I'm checking the place," Jesse murmured quietly before he disappeared.

Okay, so she was going to be the good cop, and he could be the bad cop. Or she figured that was what he wanted to do—until the real cops showed up.

"Can you tell me what happened? We know you didn't want to hurt anyone, but you're on video leaving that backpack." She figured specifics would get him to open up more.

Sniffling, he sat up, still clutching the pillow to his middle. "My mom is sick, has late-stage Alzheimer's. It's why I've been working so many hours, but the bills are piling up. Even with her insurance..." He shuddered, closed his eyes. "They offered to cover all her bills, everything, to put her in an even nicer place. All I had to do was...leave the backpack."

He couldn't say "leave the bomb," she noticed. Wasn't sure he'd ever be able to own what he'd done. Maybe after the shock had worn off he would. She was glad he was in shock though, because she had a feeling it was the only reason he was talking so freely.

"You did a little more than that though. Do you know how they managed to hack into the security system?"

With a miserable nod, he said, "Yeah, that was me. I brought donuts to the security room and plugged a USB into the port they indicated."

Well, that'd do it.

"Who is *they*? And what do they want?" She tried to keep calm, to keep her questions short and answerable so he would stay focused.

"I don't actually know. Just some guy. At first I thought it was a competitor or something when the guy approached me."

"Where did he approach you?"

"Ah...a bar I go to every Thursday night. They've got karaoke." He sniffed harder now as he appeared to struggle holding back another wave of tears.

Jesse stepped into the living room again, but thankfully hung back. She'd never seen him this angry, couldn't believe he'd kicked the door in, but she wasn't surprised. This asshole had planted a bomb in a place where a lot of people could have been hurt. What if someone had forgotten something, returned and...

She had to shelve those thoughts, especially since they'd almost died. "What does he look like?"

"Ah, boring, I guess." Beeker's gaze flicked behind her to Jesse's, then he looked away again, fear flickering in his dark eyes. "White guy, brown hair, I think. He always wore a ball cap, but yeah, brown hair."

"Always" indicated that they'd met more than once. "How many times did you two meet?"

"Only twice. The first time when he approached me about taking care of my mom. And the second when..." He closed his eyes again, but at least he managed to keep it together. "When he gave me the USB and bag. Mr. Lennox," he blurted, opening his eyes, "I'm so sorry. I can't... Everything just snowballed, but I should have come to you. Her bills were piling up and..."

He continued rambling a nonsensical apology, but she could hear sirens in the distance. Time was running out.

"Can you remember the name of the bar?"

"Yeah, it's right off King Street in Alexandria." He rambled off the name and even the address of the place.

"Do you remember the dates?"

"Yeah." His tone was dejected as he gave them. Then he looked up at Jesse again, his expression pleading. "You've got to believe me—"

"You planted a bomb, David. A *bomb*. Where you work. Where other people work, people you supposedly care about. I don't have to believe anything."

That started another round of sobs, and yep, they were done. Hailey stood and headed for the front door with Jesse in tow, without another word.

"I called Special Agent Parker, but he was already on the way," Jesse said as they headed for the stairs instead of the elevators.

The sirens were piercing the air now, only dimming slightly when they stepped into the stairwell. "I'm all for fleeing the scene but...should we wait?"

Jesse looked at her as they descended. "We were ordered to stay, but it's up to you."

She grinned a little maniacally. "Forget that. How much cash do you have on you?"

He blinked. "Ah, I don't know. A couple thousand."

"Okay, let's head to the karaoke bar and see if you can get a copy of the security feeds before the Feds swoop in."

"Pretty sure you could just hack into the system," he murmured as they reached the bottom of the stairs. Instead of heading out to the lobby, they exited through a side door that dumped them right out into the main parking lot.

"Just be casual," she said as two cop cars pulled to a stop in front of the building.

He remained still with her, using the shadows to maintain cover as the cops hurried into the lobby.

She waited a few beats to make sure they were inside, then said, "Let's go."

"Do you avoid cops often?" he asked once they were in the safety and warmth—and absolute plushness—of his SUV.

"Not really, probably because I don't usually kick doors in." She gave him a sideways look, her tone pointed. "And not that I'm trying to reward bad behavior, but that display of rage was sort of hot."

He let out a startled bark of laughter. "The caveman thing do it for you?"

No, but *he* did it for her. Always had. In response, she just snorted.

CHaPTer 17

"What the hell is going on?" Henry hissed quietly into his phone. "This was supposed to be taken care of." He nodded at one of his golfing buddies—one who was currently sleeping with his wife's best friend—and strode outside the simple brasserie.

"When I arrived, the cops and Feds were already there, walking him out. But I'll handle Beeker." His fixer's voice was low, but he could hear the sounds of traffic in the background, as if the other man was walking.

"It might be too late unless he offs himself." And Beeker was supposed to have been taken care of right after the bombing. "What does he know? And why weren't you there earlier?"

"He doesn't know anything that can point to either of us. He doesn't know my name, certainly doesn't know anything about you. Even if he tells the cops what happened, it won't matter. Nothing will come back on you. Because you hire me for a reason."

"That still doesn't explain why you weren't there earlier."

"I *was* there, waiting for him, but he never came back, so I followed the tracker in his phone to that same bar he always goes to. He wasn't there when I arrived, so I waited around to see if he showed up looking for his phone. When he didn't, I went back to his place. Everything is fine."

He took a deep breath, nodded to himself. "You're right." Then another thought occurred to him. "What about the bar you guys met up at? Any link to you there?"

"No, it's his local watering hole. And I paid the bartender to lose the security feed from both times we met. Guy made an easy grand for doing almost nothing. Just trust me."

Henry did trust him. He was simply agitated because he wanted what was in Easton Reed's head. The man was currently at his new safe house sleeping, but in the morning he was going to start helping them or pay a hefty price.

Everything was fine. Henry had to keep reminding himself of that. He had things under control. And once he had Reed's research, he'd be set for life. He could dump his wife and live the life he wanted. Everyone thought he was just a "pretty face," but he knew what he was doing right now.

He simply had to be patient, something he usually hated. But for this amount of money and a chance to live the life he wanted, he could do anything at all.

CHAPTER 18

—You are either on my side, by my side, or in my way.—

"This place isn't too bad. Decent enough security." Hailey glanced around the interior of the bar as she and Jesse strode inside.

Brick walls, high ceilings, vintage-style paintings all set a mood along with the dim lighting and sleek wood bar area lined with barstools—most of them occupied. The lighting of the place set off a soft glow, really helping people work those beer goggles. Most of the high-top tables were filled as well, and there was a rowdy bunch near the stage where someone was singing karaoke.

They headed to the bar area instead, took two of the only free chairs. Luckily, it seemed most people were turned toward the stage where someone was doing a terrible Tina Turner rendition. The woman had been a queen, and there were some songs that no mere mortals should ever try to mimic. Doing her best to tune out what could only be called noise, Hailey scanned the bar, Jesse right next to her.

"How do you want to handle this?" she asked him as a bartender with a charming, toothy grin approached. She didn't like him on sight.

"What can I get for the two of you?" His grin was firmly in place, which, yeah, made sense since the guy was in a customer-facing role. But his vibe was all wrong, and if there was one thing she'd learned growing up in the system—and in a war zone, trying not to get her ass blown up—it was to trust her gut.

Jesse placed a wad of cash on the bar, palm up. Oh wow, the man was just getting right to the heart of it, something she could appreciate. Sometimes a situation didn't need finesse, but an angry hammer. "I've got two grand for you if you can give me a copy of some of your security feeds."

The guy eyed them both, scanning her quickly, then looking Jesse over with a discerning eye, his gaze lingering on Jesse's watch. "You a cop?"

They both made scoffing sounds.

"Do we look like cops?" Jesse's tone was dry.

The bartender's gaze flicked to the cash before Jesse tucked it away. "What security feeds?"

Jesse gave him the dates.

And something in the guy's eyes flickered with a sort of *knowing*. "Someone already paid me to destroy the feeds from those dates. And since my boss is a cheap ass, our feeds are local, not sent off to a company. We just use some standard shit ordered online."

Well, this has been a bust.

"But..." He eyed that watch again. "He was shady, so I kept the downloads just in case. So. That watch for the recordings."

Hailey blinked at the balls on the guy. The watch was worth at least twenty grand. In the big scheme of things, Easton's life was worth a hell of a lot more than that. But this asshole couldn't know that.

Jesse didn't pause, simply slipped the watch off and slid it across the bar.

The bartender blinked in clear surprise, then his gaze grew calculating.

Oh, hell no. "If you try to renegotiate, I'll burn this bar down with you in it." Hailey's voice was low, blade sharp.

The man looked at her in surprise, as if he'd forgotten she was there. Then he took her in, really looked her over, and whatever he saw in her face must have convinced him of the truth. He glanced down at the other bartender. "Cover me for a few, Kelly Ann." Then he looked back at them. "Give me five."

"If he runs off with that watch..." She gritted her teeth, not bothering to finish that sentence because really, there wasn't much she'd actually do. Her only concern was finding Easton safe and sound.

"She's pretty good." Jesse chin-nodded to the stage.

"What?" Frowning, she looked past him at the barely dressed woman singing a song often performed in strip clubs. "She's terrible."

He just shrugged and gave her a ghost of a grin.

She narrowed her eyes at him. "Are you talking about something other than her voice?"

"Jealous?"

"Maybe."

He blinked in surprise, then grinned. "I was just trying to distract you. She's got assets I'm sure, but singing isn't one of them."

"The crowd of men at the front table disagrees," she said, snickering as they started whooping loudly. Did one of them just throw money on stage?

"That guy's gonna ask for your cash too." She knew it was coming as soon as the bartender returned.

If he returned.

"I know. Not that I care about the cash, but I already separated out half of it because screw this guy." Jesse's jaw ticked, and for the first time she saw the annoyance in his expression.

And she didn't think it was about the watch, but the bartender himself. Glancing at her phone, she frowned. "He should be back by now..." She trailed off as the guy pushed through the swinging door to the back, which was presumably the kitchen.

His expression was more reserved now as he showed that he was holding a USB, then slid it across the bar. "Sorry it took a bit. I added the feed from earlier tonight as well. The guy who originally asked me to delete the feeds was in here tonight, but he didn't come up to the bar. He sat at one of the back booths and tried to be incognito. Probably would have worked, but I remembered him from before.

Plus I'm good with faces. So." He shrugged. And he also didn't ask for the cash, probably realizing he'd pushed hard enough.

To her surprise, Jesse slid a folded wad of cash across the bar. "Thank you for your time. If this doesn't have what we asked for—"

"It does, I swear." The guy held his hands up, palms facing them, all easy charm.

Jesse simply nodded, then wrapped his arm around her shoulders before they headed out into the crisp night air.

Once they got into the SUV, she plugged the USB into her laptop. She had a program that isolated unknown hardware and media, so she wasn't worried about this thing corrupting her computer if the guy was trying to scam them.

As Jesse drove, she fast-forwarded through the first video, looking for Beeker. Luckily the guy wasn't trying to hide from the cameras, and it was clear he was a well-known customer when the bartender slid a beer in front of him before he'd ordered. She kept the feed moving until a man in a ball cap approached. The guy didn't say anything at first, just ordered a beer—same as Beeker's—then waited before striking up a conversation.

There was no volume on the video, but she could see the moment Beeker's body language changed, stiffened. Using a program, she pulled various angles of the man's face, then moved on to the next video and grabbed more angles. There were a couple from the exterior when the guy arrived, but he'd been looking down so nothing good.

"I'm not sure if I'll be able to use this," she murmured, realizing she hadn't said anything in a while and they were almost back to Jesse's place. "But I put together what this guy's face might look like. He was really skilled at looking down, keeping his face turned more toward the ground than anything, but I was able to pull some angles and compile something. I'll run it through our facial recognition program. And if I don't get a hit, I'll expand and use some others."

"Don't bother. I think I know who that is. Name's Adam Berch. He's essentially a fixer for Senator Henry Silva."

CHAPTER 19

—No one ever expects to fall in love.—

Cash stepped into Jesse's office, found Reese and Elijah working—well, Reese was. Elijah was leaned back in his chair, his eyes closed. Cash cleared his throat lightly to alert her to his presence.

Then Elijah jerked forward. "Don't shave my eyebrows!"

Reese snickered, and Cash paused. "I won't shave your eyebrows, promise."

"Go get some sleep, Eli. You're not doing anyone any good. You've been working your ass off today. Go recharge."

"Yeah, okay." He squeezed her shoulder once in a familiar way, one that looked brotherly.

Cash hoped it was anyway. "Did you eat dinner?"

She still didn't look up. "I ate a protein bar."

Yeah, that was what he thought. He'd done a little sleuthing—aka he'd simply texted Hailey—and found out what Reese's favorites were. "I brought you something."

She still didn't look over, even as he sat in Elijah's vacated seat.

"It's Swedish chocolate cake."

She froze for a moment, then side-eyed him, those gorgeous green eyes widening when they landed on what was in his hand. She grabbed for it. "Why didn't you lead with that?"

"So food is the way to your heart?"

She snorted even as she grabbed the fork from his other hand. "Did you make this?"

"Ah, no." But he was planning to learn if this made her that happy. Not to mention the moan she let out after her first bite. It was straight-up orgasmic. Holy shit, if he ever convinced her to take a chance on him, he'd bring chocolate cake to bed with them to sweeten the deal.

Not that women usually needed anything to sweeten the deal when it came to him. They were always throwing themselves at him. Most of it, he was fairly certain, stemmed from his money. Because he had a lot of it, thanks to his foresight in investing in Jesse. Everything the man touched turned to gold, so it just made good sense to invest in him.

"I got it from a local bakery, and there's more in the fridge."

"I take back everything bad I said about you." She grinned around a mouthful of cake.

"Why would you say anything bad about me?"

She snickered once. "I'm just kidding, man. I mean, I think it's weird how you're always smiling, but I try not to judge."

Whatever, she liked it. "So any luck on the lawyer?" Cash knew what she was working on, courtesy of Jesse and Hailey. And since he'd felt useless here, he'd gone to the office and caught up on a few things. Better than sitting around watching everyone else work on finding Easton. He hated all of this, wished he could help somehow. The man was one of his best, oldest friends.

"A little, yeah. I've compiled a fairly comprehensive file on the guy and have a list of all his clients. Or most of them anyway. I might not have all. It at least narrows down who we're looking for and why."

"Does that list include Senator Silva?"

"Yeah, why?" She polished off the last bite with another moan he felt all the way to his core.

He finished reading an incoming text from Hailey, saw she'd sent it to Reese too, but the woman must not have her phone on her. "Hailey just texted the two of us. Found a potential lead. The guy Beeker met with, the one who paid him to place that bomb." Something Cash was going to be pissed about for a long time. "He's supposedly a fixer for the senator. At least according to Jesse."

He and Jesse might have the same kind of money, but Jesse ran in very different circles than Cash did. Of course, some parts of their professional lives overlapped, but not often. Usually when they were invited to the same galas or parties. Cash almost always ignored those things, but Jesse went because the man knew how to network. Cash would rather stab himself with a fork, repeatedly, than get dressed up and go to those events. He preferred to simply donate instead.

"Oh shit, my phone," Reese murmured, looking around. Then she stood and grabbed her phone from the charger on the other side of the room.

And Cash tried not to watch her ass as she walked. Failed. Because it truly was a perfect ass. "So, do you dye your hair other colors than pink?"

Surprised, she glanced at him as she headed back to her seat. "Wanna know a secret?"

That involved her? "Always."

"They're just clip-ins. I love my hair too much to bleach then dye it." She grinned. "It feels really vain to even admit that, but whatever. My hair's way too dark to dye, so I'd have to hire my hairdresser to bleach sections, and I just can't do it." She ran a hand over her long tresses with a mocking flourish.

"You've got gorgeous hair. So." He shrugged. She had gorgeous everything, including her whole attitude.

Her expression was curious, and for a moment she looked as if she might say something, but then she turned back to her computer. "Thanks again for the cake. It was incredible."

Well, that was a dismissal if he'd ever heard one. Inwardly sighing, he stood. "You need anything else? Coffee, actually substantial food?"

"Nah, but thanks. I'm about to grab some shut-eye, just want to wrap up a couple things before I crash." She looked up at him suddenly, her expression sincere. "I'm sorry about your missing friend. We're going to find him."

He wanted to tell her not to make promises she couldn't keep, but he desperately wanted to believe they were going to find Easton. The world was a shitty place sometimes, and he knew more than most how fragile life was.

But deep inside, he was clinging to that hope that they'd find Easton and bring him home.

CHAPTER 20

—He took my heart, and I never got it back.—

"You need sleep." There was no give in Jesse's voice.

Hailey wanted to argue, but it was close to two. And if she wanted to function, she needed at least a few hours of sleep. "Fine." She trudged into his kitchen with him, once again struck by how massive the space was. "You need a dog," she murmured. To greet him when he came home every day. He'd always talked about how he wanted one.

He glanced at her in surprise as he opened the fridge, pulled out a fruit drink packed with nutrients, and handed it to her. "Drink this. You'll thank me later. And one day I might get one. I've definitely thought about it."

He was holding back something. She could see it because she knew him. It didn't matter that time stretched between them, he wanted to say more. "I'm surprised you don't have one. You always talked about it." There was a melancholy note to his voice.

Probably because they'd talked about it together. After drinking half the bottle, she set it down on the countertop, already feeling a little more refreshed. "I tried to get one," she confessed. "Went to a shelter and started crying because I couldn't take them all home. I ended up running out of there like a total loon and never went back."

Jesus, she'd never told anyone that story—it was beyond embarrassing. And the only reason she could think that she was telling him was because she was exhausted.

Yep. That was the reason. Exhaustion.

Wordlessly, he closed the distance between them and pulled her into his arms.

And she didn't hesitate. She buried her face against his chest, glad to hold onto him, especially at this time. And to her surprise, she felt another set of arms come around them, looked up, and saw it was Cash. She hadn't even known he was there.

But she could see the glistening in his eyes and realized that, duh, this was hitting him just as hard as them. "We're gonna find him," she murmured, shifting her arm so that she was hugging them both. "And for the record, because I'm so tired I can barely think straight, I've missed you guys so much."

But Jesse the most. Her voice cracked on the last word, and she turned into Jesse again, unable to stop the swift rush of unexpected tears. Cash kissed the top of her head, then murmured that he was going to crash before she found herself being lifted up by Jesse.

"I can walk," she mumbled even as he scooped her up, then placed the fruit drink in her hand.

"I know, but I can carry you just as easily. Now drink."

"You're bossy tonight."

"Yep. It's my turn to be bossy, so get used to it."

"I kinda like it." Did she say that out loud?

"Probably the only time you'll ever admit that," he murmured.

She realized he was carrying her into his room and shifted slightly in his arms.

"I picked my room so when you run away in the morning, you can retreat to your room instead of your friend's." His tone was only a little dry.

"I didn't run." Yep, that was petulance in her voice as he set her on her feet.

As he made a grunt of disagreement, she finished the fruit drink, surprised by how much it refreshed her. Today had been...*long* seemed like an understatement.

As she set the bottle down on a coaster—she loved that he had them, because of course he did—she strode to the bank of windows overlooking the pool and backyard. Talk about a view.

Lots of space, which of course he would want after having none growing up. A lush green yard even in the winter, a huge pool, a pool house, covered seating on the lanai with Edison-style lights, and what looked like a small greenhouse lit up in the distance.

She watched his reflection in the glass as he approached, automatically leaned back into him as he wrapped his arms around her. She'd missed these arms, missed every single thing about Jesse Lennox.

"You're staying in here tonight."

"I know." That wasn't even a question. And at the end of the day—any day, of any year, for the rest of time—she could never regret sleeping with him. "I just don't want *you* to regret anything."

"You don't know me as well as you think you do if you think I could ever regret you."

"Jesse—"

"No." He turned her in his arms, his expression intense as he cupped her face. "Right now is just about you and me. Nothing else. And I'm going down on you because I've been thinking about it for a long time."

"I wanted to go down on you first," she whispered, feeling her cheeks warm up. She'd been thinking about it too, which felt kind of messed up.

"Not now."

"That's not fair." She rubbed her hand over his covered erection, shuddered at the feel of how hard he was, how thick. Oh, she'd missed him in more ways than one.

"You can beg for it later." His eyes glinted mischievously, a hint of wicked in them.

Okay, that was way too hot. "Can you, like, cover your windows? I'm worried some of your guards will see us or something," she murmured as she ran her palm over his erection again. Squeezed once.

He groan-laughed and eased away for a moment, pressed a button on a remote control, and moments later automatic curtains rolled into place, blocking out the world. "No one gets to see what's mine," he growled, stalking toward her again.

But she wasn't his.

As if he read her mind, his eyes narrowed. "Oh, but you are, Hailey. Always have been. So get used to it. You ran away last time, and I couldn't follow. I'll hunt you to Antarctica if there is a next time."

"Jesse—"

"I only want to hear my name on your lips if it's, 'oh Jesse, yes, make me come,' or 'harder.' That's it, Kitten." He tugged off his shirt as he reached her, tossed it to the floor even as he claimed her mouth with his.

And he was definitely claiming her. More than he realized. Or maybe he knew exactly what he was doing because his declaration had her stunned into silence.

Also, the way he was tangling his tongue with hers did a good job of that too.

She wanted to take her time with him since they'd been so fast and furious on the plane, but she was still desperate to get him naked. To touch and stroke him anywhere she pleased. As she worked the buckle of his pants, he did the same for her, managing to shove them off. And as she stepped out of hers, he grasped the hem of her shirt, guiding it up and off her, his fingers skimming over her hips, waist, barely covered breasts.

She unhooked her bra before he could do it, and the next thing she knew, he'd scooped her up again. She wasn't in the habit of letting anyone carry her around, but she'd always make an exception for him.

"What are you doing?" she asked, but quickly realized as he stepped into the bathroom—which was bigger than her bedroom back home.

"Taking care of you," was his simple answer.

Simple or not, it destroyed her, driving home the point that no one had ever measured up to him and never would. She'd never even tried to move on, and in this moment she knew why. *Truly* understood it. Jesse had stolen part of her heart years ago, and she'd never gotten it back. Never wanted it back, because at least it meant that he had part of her. That she'd struck a claim on him, even if she couldn't have all of him.

But she was so greedy, and in this moment, she desperately wanted all of him.

As he started the shower, she slid her hands up his bare chest, trailing her fingers over the sharp indents of his muscles. Whatever his workout routine was, Navy SEALs should take note because holy shit.

When they'd been in the plane, things had been so fast that she hadn't paid attention to the tattoos on his arms. But as she trailed her fingers over the one on his upper left bicep, she froze. "What is this?" she whispered.

"What does it look like?" His eyes were challenging as he looked down at her, the water from the overhead rain shower the perfect pulsing beat of warmth.

Staring, trying to make sense, she saw that the intricate script that created a heart was made up of... "Dates." And as she read the first one, her throat tightened in emotion. The first day they'd met—the day she'd threatened him. The next was their first kiss, then the first time they'd had sex (those were close together), then...the day she'd left him.

She blinked away the onslaught of tears that rushed up, threatened to drown her.

"There's still room for one more date, maybe two if the artist gets creative. It's either going to be the day you came back to me, or the day we—"

She grabbed onto his face, pulled him down, and slammed her mouth to his because she was too afraid to hear the words. They could go either way, but she knew what he'd been about to say, and she simply couldn't take it.

Not right now.

If she did, she'd fracture into a million little pieces.

He grasped onto her ass and backed her up to the slick tiled wall as the water pounded down around them. Then he cupped her mound, searching, teasing with one, then two fingers.

He was gentle at first, then when he found how slick she already was, he groaned again, slid his fingers deep inside her. "I wanted to go down on you first."

"Later." Because she had no patience for self-control now. "After the shower. Inside me now." She needed him in her, was hungry for the way he filled her, stretched her—consumed all of her.

He made a strangled sound of maybe frustration or desire—she wasn't certain as he lifted her up. Maybe both.

His erection was so hard that she slid right onto him, the tension that had been building inside her snapping free before a new kind of tension built right back up.

She arched her back as he filled her, savored the sensation of being stretched by him. "Jesse," she moaned. "You feel amazing."

"Whose pussy is this?" he growled, pinning her in place, refusing to let her roll her hips, to gain any buildup for what she needed to find release.

Her inner walls clenched around him as she tried to move.

"Whose?" He stared down at her, his chest rising and falling in agitation.

"Yours." A one-word confession that wasn't a confession at all. Just the raw truth.

"That's right." Triumph lit his blue eyes as he pulled back slowly, then pushed inside her in a sharp thrust that had her arching her body into him.

She lost all sense of time as they both let go of control, became the most primal parts of themselves.

It had always been like this with him, and as he thrust over and over, her climax built with intensity, that burning need inside her climbing until finally she knew she was close.

As he cupped one of her breasts, pinched her nipple with more intensity than she'd expected but found she loved, she bit his bottom lip. "Gonna come." It was about all she could squeeze out.

He growled something that might have been "good," but she wasn't sure as he reached between their bodies. When he teased her clit, rubbing the sensitive bundle of nerves into oblivion, she let go of the last thin shred of her self-control.

And as she came, he let go too, growling against her mouth as he slammed her up against the tile. The sensation of her breasts rubbing against his chest intensified her pleasure as he lost himself inside her.

By the time she came back to reality, he was easing out of her, helping her to her feet. Thankfully he held on to her, because her knees barely held her up.

Taking her by surprise, he nudged her under the rainfall, and as soon as her hair was soaked, started gently washing her hair. The scent of his shampoo was familiar—the same as hers. She wasn't even sure how he had the same brand as she did, but she leaned her head back and let him take care of her, enjoying the feel of his fingers against her scalp, her body.

He did the same with her conditioner, then washed her entire body in slow, methodic strokes before he quickly took care of his own. And as he turned the water off, she knew she needed to do something, but he took over there too.

And she let him, didn't even question herself as he took charge, drying her hair, then her body, and carrying her to his bed.

Because this man had always taken care of her.

CHAPTER 21

—She took my heart, and I don't want it back.—

As she slowly came awake, Jesse slid between Hailey's legs, gently pushing them open. She'd needed the sleep, so when she'd crashed hard in his bed after their shower, he'd simply curled up around her and held her close.

"What are you doing?" she murmured, her voice thick with sleep.

"Tasting you." *Finally.* They'd both slept naked, which was just perfect.

"Oh." She let out a little moan as she slid her fingers through his hair. "You feel good." Her voice was still sleepy, that in-between state, but as he slid his tongue along her folds she rolled her hips against his face, moaning louder.

Yeah, she was waking up.

And he'd missed doing this, missed all of her. They'd missed out on too many years together. And if she wanted to run again, fine.

He'd simply catch her.

"Jesse." Her legs trembled around his head as he slid a finger inside her, working her up. Though she was already wet from his teasing.

He pressed her thighs open and continued stroking her, loving how reactive she was. With each flick of his tongue, then stroke of his fingers, he knew she was getting closer.

And when he sucked on her clit with no warning, she nearly jolted off the bed with a cry of pleasure. He grinned against her, sucked again.

She made an incoherent moan that sounded a lot like "please, more," so he increased the pressure on the little bundle of nerves until she was climaxing against his face and fingers.

Her orgasm hit hard, the feel of it coating his fingers as she came down from her high. She stared down the length of her body at him, a soft smile on her face. "You can wake me up like that anytime."

Oh, he was going to take her up on that.

"Now get inside me," she murmured, already reaching for him.

And she didn't have to ask him twice. He crawled up her body, reveling in the fact that she'd woken up in his bed. That she was here after all their years apart.

"I have morning breath," she murmured, grinning at him as he positioned himself between her spread thighs.

"Don't care." He claimed her mouth even as he slid deep inside her. Didn't care at all. After they left his bedroom, they'd be back at the investigation so he was going to take these stolen moments with her.

"You feel so good." Her words were garbled against his mouth as she arched her back against him, meeting him stroke for stroke.

He wanted to tell her that he felt the same, but the words stuck in his throat as pleasure built inside him. She was so tight, her inner walls clenching around him with each thrust.

As they lost themselves inside each other, she clutched onto him with a ferocity he felt to his core. He gripped onto her hips, and as he told himself to calm down and hold back, she dug her fingers into his ass.

"I'm going to come again." She sounded surprised, but he was glad.

Because he was about to come too. He nipped her bottom lip, bit down. "Come for me *now*."

Her entire body jolted at his words, and he could feel her let go, just give in to the pleasure. So he did the same, coming hard inside her, the only place he ever wanted to find release.

As they came back to themselves, he hated to pull out of her but eased out and grabbed a washcloth from the bathroom. After he'd taken care of her, he slid back into bed, pulled her close.

They needed to get out of bed, to get moving, but he couldn't force his arms to loosen as she laid her head on his chest.

"Only five more minutes," she murmured as if she'd read his mind. Or in reality was on the same wavelength as him. Because they had shit to do.

Jesse had half a dozen missed calls on his cell phone from the special agent in charge of Easton's investigation—likely because he'd boldly kicked in Beeker's door in full view of the security camera. But no one had shown up on his doorstep yet. Or if they had, his security hadn't told him.

Not that he was concerned much with the agent. No, he had something different on his mind.

"Why'd you leave me?" he murmured against the top of Hailey's head, knowing it could destroy this small spell around them. But he needed the truth. If they were going to forge a future, it had to be based on truth. They had to put the past behind them.

To his surprise, she didn't pull away. She simply sighed into his chest. "Because I would have held you back, Jesse."

He blinked, then frowned. "What the hell are you talking about?"

"That right there is why I left. Jesus, don't you remember what I was like? I'd gotten arrested a few times. I only finished high school because you pushed me, and you were going off to *Harvard*." She leaned back now, her expression unreadable. "I would have just dragged you down when you needed to focus on school, on your *future*. You'd already created some amazing stuff. You didn't need me." She looked away, but didn't try to leave, thankfully.

Even though he was angry, he gathered her back against him as he tried to find the right words. "That's bullshit," he murmured, holding her close. "I believe that *you* believe what you just said, but it's still bullshit."

She sniffled once. "You say that because we were horny teenagers."

"Well, I'm not a horny teenager now, and I can see with clarity that you wouldn't have dragged anyone down. Because, yes, I remember *exactly* what you were like. You were the life of our group, Hailey. You forced Easton to make friends, to push past his comfort zone, and I still see that in him today. With Cash, you protected him even when he swore he didn't need it. You were the perfect sounding board and knew when to give advice and when to just listen. And with me..." He swore softly, trying to find the right words. "You were my biggest supporter. I felt like I could do *anything* with you around because you were convinced I could do anything." She'd given him the confidence he hadn't had before her.

"You *can* do anything," she muttered. "You're basically a creative genius."

"Don't run from me, from all of us, again. Please, Hailey."

"I'll try not to. I just... you don't know everything about me, Jesse. If I'd stayed, I'd have ruined things between us, trust me."

Yeah, that sounded like a bunch of bullshit from her now-deceased mother's mouth. But he didn't say that. He had demons of his own in the form of dead, addict parents. "You wouldn't have ruined anything, and I don't need to know everything about you. I know the important stuff." He kissed the top of her head, inhaled her familiar scent.

A short rap on the door made them pause.

"Yeah?" Jesse called out, even as he realized a small weight had been lifted from his chest.

"Breakfast is almost ready," Cash said. "And Hailey, your computer is making sounds. Thought you might want to check them out."

"Hell," she muttered, pulling out of Jesse's arms in clear regret. "We've got to get back to it."

"I know. Just...talk to me if you're feeling like running."

"Okay."

The anvil on his chest eased slightly but not fully as he watched her slide from his bed and gather her discarded clothes.

Because he wasn't sure if she was telling the truth or not. Either way, he wasn't letting her run again.

CHAPTER 22

Seven years ago

Hailey,

I still think about you more than I should admit. I'm not certain how much news you see, but I've come up with some new apps recently I hope will be beneficial for you and your friends. Stay safe.

—Jesse

***

Hey Hailey,

I head out today to places unknown. Not really, but I can't tell you where, something I know you understand. Boot camp wasn't as bad as I thought, which makes me think I'm jinxing myself now. But compared to some of the shit I dealt with as a kid, *yawn*. And isn't that a ringing endorsement for our foster system? Imagine me rolling my gorgeous eyes.

Did you send me some care packages? I got a few that both Jesse and Easton deny sending, and I can't imagine why they'd lie. Plus there was a whole box of black jelly beans—and I know you hate them. Almost felt like a spite gift for all the times I called you assface. But since there was also a bunch of cookies, I forgive you. And if you didn't send them, then I have a stalker with weird taste. Whatever, one of my friends ate the jelly beans. So at least they weren't wasted. Unless you count when he puked them up later after a night out. Barf.

Still miss your dumbass self, and thanks for the packages. I knew you still cared. Easton broke up with his latest boyfriend and has once again thrown himself into work. Well, not once again. He never actually stopped being a workaholic. If I had a brain that big, I'd use it to make billions, buy a yacht or an island, and never talk to anyone again. But what he's doing is cool too. Saving the world and all with his research. Probably better that he gets that brain. It balances out, considering my good looks. And yes, I can practically see you rolling your eyes. I know the truth is hard to swallow. Being handsome is simply my cross to bear.

Not sure where you are, but maybe we'll cross paths in the future. Watch your six, short stuff.

—Cash

***

Hailey,

Cash leaves soon, and I'm going to miss him terribly. He's going somewhere overseas by way of California. For the first time in years, I see a spark in him. So even though I'm selfish enough to wish he would stay near Jesse and me, I'm happy for him. Cash needs a different kind of challenge than school. This life is too calm for him. I hope he finds what he's looking for. (Just as I hope you've found what you're looking for).

He always jokes about being the dumb one, but it's nonsense. I've seen him break apart a car engine to fix something, then put it back together with an impressive ease. The man is just too stubborn to see what's right in front of him sometimes.

I'm moving to the Virginia area soon, and I've included my new address. I'm not there quite yet, but my new place is all set up, and it's a far cry from college life or anything before. It feels strange to want to put down roots, but that's what I'm going to do.

I tried dating again, but I think it's not for me. At least not right now. I'm excited about my new job and have already worked with some of the people before, so I won't be going in blind at least. I know it shouldn't matter, but it eases some of that anxiety I worry I'll never get rid of.

I still miss you, and even though you don't respond, I hold you and our memories close to my heart. And as always, I'm here if you want to talk.

Sincerely,
Easton

CHAPTER 23

"So this is Adam Berch." Hailey leaned back in her chair and nodded at the wall screen. "No social media accounts, and six whole pictures I've managed to find of him online. All with him turned to the side. These don't include the video clips from the other night at the bar where he met Beeker."

"He hired someone to scrub his online presence," Reese murmured. "And whoever did it, did an incredible job. I couldn't even find online high school photos or anything."

"If his school never digitized, it would make sense." Because Berch was in his forties, owned a townhome outright in a very expensive area, and had a murky job description. He worked for Senator Silva as a consultant, but he was a fixer essentially. "I did manage to get his military records. Dishonorable discharge from the army, but the reasons why aren't clear. So he's got some training and he's been working for Silva long enough that he's obviously valued. I think if we follow him, we'll find Easton. He's the link between the bombing and Beeker. Also," she said, clearing her throat, "I gave his picture to Hazel."

Reese's eyes widened slightly. "For real?"

"I want to stay as transparent as possible, because no matter my feelings about the Feds, they do have good resources. Maybe they'll find something we haven't."

"Senator Silva is going to be at a fundraiser tonight," Jesse said, looking up from his phone, his gaze on Hailey as he spoke. "My assistant just sent me the guest list

I requested. He's on it. I'd planned to simply donate, but if Silva is going to this fundraiser, we could too."

She tried to ignore what his looks did to her. What his mere presence did to her. She had to be one hundred percent focused right now to find Easton.

"Yeah, I got an invite to that thing too," Cash murmured. "I'd planned to skip, but we could all go."

Hailey nodded slowly. "We could potentially plant a tracker on the senator's vehicle. Or more importantly, clone his phone. Hell, we could clone Berch's phone if he's there. Do you remember seeing him at functions with Silva before? You're the one who recognized him."

"Not at a function like this, no. Not inside anyway. I remember seeing him once or twice waiting for the senator as he left, and his expression was always intense."

"Since I haven't been able to find his phone number or anything that gives me a way to track the guy, I'm down to go tonight if there's a possibility he'll be there."

"Me too," Reese agreed, though she didn't look happy about it. But she quickly pivoted as she turned to her own laptop. "So, Ian Warren is definitely involved in this shit. He's set up too many shell corporations for the senator—and a lot of other political figures in DC—not to be. He's helping the senator funnel his money into this big pharma research. And I'm not a hundred percent certain, but I'm pretty sure he's using his campaign funds. If we can prove that..." She let out a whistle. "We could blackmail the asshole into letting Easton go."

"He's also cheating on his wife," Elijah added. "But I don't think anyone in DC or anywhere would really care too much. And I don't think we can use that against him."

"It might hit the news for a while, but you're right." Jesse nodded. "The senator is known for not being able to keep it in his pants. I almost guarantee his wife knows what he's up to, and I don't know that the senator would care enough to hide it."

"It's still knowledge we can hold on to," Hailey said. "Use it later if we need it. Who's he cheating with?" Elijah had sent her a file on it, but she hadn't had a chance to look it over since waking up and grabbing a quick breakfast.

"Ah, her name's Chloe Grace. From Elijah's profile, she looks like a pro."

"She's one of the best. She's a very high-priced escort. Discreet, professional, you'll never get anything from her," Cash said.

Reese lifted an eyebrow at him. "You know her personally?"

Cash grinned. "Did some work for her—*construction* work. But she offered her other services free of charge for me." And he looked stupidly pleased with himself.

"I'm sure you'd have paid in other ways," Hailey murmured, shaking her head at him. "Okay, so she's a pro. That's a good thing. We might be able to get information from her if we speak the right language."

"What's that?" Cash asked.

"Money," Jesse said before Hailey could respond.

"Okay, so are you opposed to approaching her? Since she knows you?" Hailey asked Cash. "See if you can get some dirt on the senator."

"I'm not opposed to it, but I'm telling you she won't give us anything."

"And we might tip our hand." Reese frowned as she looked back at her screen. "But maybe we could approach her a different way."

Hailey tapped her finger on the desk in front of her, then looked up at Jesse. "Maybe you could approach her, then. For like...I don't know, a 'date.' Proposition her for a discreet business agreement. Then plant something at her place. Or clone her phone. Whatever."

Cash snorted, drawing everyone's attention to him. "No way. He's a monk, and like I said, she's a pro. She'll sniff out something weird."

Jesse simply shrugged. "He's not wrong. She won't believe me."

"And I'm a known commodity. It should be me who contacts her," Cash said.

"Okay, so you approach as wanting to hire her, or as wanting blackmail on someone. Someone not the senator," Hailey said.

"Yeah," Reese murmured, working on her computer. "We've got a few pictures of her with different men and women in the DC area. You could just pick one of them and offer her a lot of money for information on them. And then either clone her phone or plant something at her place."

"We can try," Cash murmured. "I just feel like she'll be prepared for something like that."

Hailey ran a hand down her face. "You're probably not wrong. Someone like that is going to be a hell of a lot more careful than some of the dumbasses she sees."

"I'll approach her though," Cash continued. "See what I can find out. Maybe we'll get lucky."

"It's worth a shot," Reese murmured.

"You're coming with me," Cash said, not looking up from his phone as he texted.

"Wait...who are you talking to?" Hailey asked. "And what do you mean?"

Cash looked up now, but not at Hailey. "Reese, you're coming with me to talk to Chloe Grace. We'll approach her as a couple looking to spice up our love life."

Reese made a barfing sound, but then rolled her eyes. "Fine, whatever. But we've also got to get some dresses for the gala tonight. If we're going to do this thing, we need to look the part."

"I'm taking care of that." Now Jesse was pulling out his phone again. "Or rather my assistant is," he said as he held his phone up to his ear.

Hailey listened as he quickly made plans to have dresses delivered for both of them as well as having a makeup artist and hair stylist come by a couple hours before the gala.

"That was impressive," Hailey murmured as he hung up.

"Not really." Jesse shrugged. "Just what happens when you have money."

"Well, impressive or not, it's one thing off our list. Since Cash is going to approach Ms. Grace, I say you or both of us contact that attorney. Didn't you say he'd pitched his services to you before?" Hailey asked.

"I did say that." He looked at his phone. "It's early, but he'll be up. I'll reach out, see if he's free."

"Chloe is free for us in a couple hours," Cash said as he looked up, his grin mischievous. "Maybe we should practice being a real couple before we head over."

"How about, *barf*." Reese rolled her eyes before looking at Hailey and Elijah. "Okay, so we've got a game plan. Eli, you'll back us up?"

"Yep," he murmured, not even looking at them as he opened one of their bags. "I'll get all the gear organized. You two go get ready."

And that was that. Hailey could feel the change in the air, the same as she always did when working a job. They were getting a lot closer, pulling on the threads that mattered. All they needed was a lead. A location.

And they could save Easton.

"Special Agent Parker is calling again." Jesse's tone was dry as he glanced down at his phone.

"You gonna answer?" she asked as she headed out of the office with him.

"Nope."

Okay, then. She just hoped that didn't come back to bite them in the ass later.

CHAPTER 24

—That moment you realize that she is definitely worth the risk.—

"I don't know why you needed me for this," Reese grumbled next to Cash, her arms crossed over her chest as he pulled into a curbside parking spot a block away from where they were going.

Ooh, she was grumpy. And he found he liked it way too much. "You're too tense. If you're supposed to be with me, you've got to loosen up." Cash reached out a hand across the center console, but she batted it away. "Okay, but that's the only one you get. When we get out of the car, I'm going to take your hand, and we have to be in acting mode. That's what Hailey called it, right?"

She gave him a dry look, and all he wanted to do was nibble on her bottom lip. She was ridiculously hot and adorable at the same time. She had long, blue-black hair, stunning green eyes, and curves for days. But her mouth... her mouth was everything. Both her actual, gorgeous full lips he'd had more than one fantasy about, and the actual shit that came out of said mouth.

"Yes, you're right. I've done this before. I can do it again." She straightened her shoulders as if she was going to a firing squad.

And, okay, it was hell on his ego. But it made him want her even more, which was just more testament to how screwed up he was. He checked the mirrors of his

SUV before he got out and opened her door. Smiling only a little obnoxiously at her, he took her hand as she stepped out.

She was petite but had worn four-inch heels which...still didn't do much for her height. But she fit right up against him as he slid an arm around her shoulders. Oh yeah, she fit perfectly.

Sighing, she slid her arm around him as they headed down the sidewalk. The neighborhood was quiet, filled with brick brownstones and cobblestone side-walks. And even in the winter, there was still a lot of green everywhere. Bicycles were propped up in front of some of the walkups, and expensive cars were parked curbside as they strode down the cobblestones. "So what kind of 'work' did you do for this woman?"

He snickered at her tone. "My company takes on high-end custom jobs, and she wanted a shower that could fit five people comfortably."

Now her mouth broke into a wide grin as she snickered as well. "I'm surprised you didn't take her up on her offer, then. Or was she trying to get out of paying?"

"No, this was after she'd paid. A 'bonus' she called it. And I think you'll like her, even as I reiterate that she's not going to give up anything on Silva."

"Well, we'll never know until we try." She looked up at him, sniffed in that haughty manner that almost brought him to his knees.

So he knelt down and brushed his lips against hers, only pulling back when she jolted in surprise.

"What are you doing?"

"Getting that out of the way so if I kiss you in front of her you won't jump like a scared rabbit."

"There will be no kissing in front of her. It's not like she's going to demand we bang on her living room floor before agreeing to service us."

He barked out an unexpected laugh. "You never know."

Her mouth curved up slightly, and she simply shook her head.

"This is it," he murmured.

"This is an old-money area." Her voice was low, her tone impressed as she eyed the regal looking brownstone.

He only murmured an agreement because they were almost at the door, and he knew Chloe had cameras. To his surprise, the door opened only moments after he'd pressed the electronic bell and smiled at the doorbell camera.

Chloe greeted them both with a warm, inviting smile, stepping back. "Please come in. It's been too long."

Cash greeted her with a quick hug, and Reese gave her a small, shy smile. And he didn't think Reese had a shy bone in her body, so apparently she could act.

"I was surprised to hear from you." Chloe shut and locked the door behind them. "And for the record, normally you would have gone through a long vetting process before I even contemplated bringing you on as a client. But I made an exception for you."

Reese glanced around the space, and he knew she was looking for somewhere to plant a mini camera. The bedroom would be the best place, but might not be a possibility.

"My girl here has been feeling adventurous, and I only want to keep her happy."

Chloe motioned to the plush seating in front of a fireplace. Everything was in neutral cream tones, elegant and inviting. "Please sit. And what would you like? Sparkling water, mimosas, coffee? Something else?"

"Sparkling water for me," Reese murmured. "You have a lovely home."

"Thank you. Coffee for you?"

He nodded and pulled Reese into his lap as he sat in one of the oversized chairs by the fireplace. The fire crackled quietly, the setting clearly all about comfort.

After setting the drinks on the ottoman between them, Chloe sat on the love seat across from them and crossed her long legs. Her blonde hair was pulled back in some complicated twist, her makeup was perfection, and she'd probably spent tens of thousands on her teeth. He understood why her clients were attracted to her, but everything about her was too hard and artificial. Or maybe it was because he understood how she'd grown up—similar to him.

"So," she said, "tell me why you're really here, because I don't believe for one second you want to hire me."

Reese had been in the process of reaching forward to pick up her drink, her perfect ass gliding over his cock, which he desperately needed to get under control. But she froze at Chloe's words, then delicately cleared her throat.

"Told you it wouldn't work," he said around a laugh, keeping his easy tone going. Because Chloe had still invited them in, which meant she was curious.

Reese sighed, then immediately moved off him—his cock was sad—and onto the seat next to him. "We need information."

Okay then, they were just going to jump into it?

Apparently Reese surprised Chloe too, because the other woman blinked. "I don't talk about my business."

"We're not interested in your business. Just one client in particular," Reese said.

"Nope." Chloe shook her head as she leaned back on her sofa. "I don't even want to know the name because it won't matter."

"A friend of Cash's has been kidnapped, and one of your clients—"

"I don't care." Chloe's tone was icy, but he saw the glint of something in her eyes. Maybe fear. Or... compassion?

He couldn't tell because Reese stood up, all indignant fire. Yep, not one shy bone in that hot body.

"Fine. Keep your secrets." Reese leaned over the ottoman and coffee table, her finger out. "But if his friend dies, and I find out you could have stopped it, you'd better run and hide. Because I will personally hold you responsible if he doesn't." She knocked over the water as she stood back up, but ignored it as she stalked out of the room toward the entryway.

"Cash, I—" Chloe started.

Cash's easy demeanor slid away as he stood as well, even as he heard the front door open, then slam. "My childhood friend has been kidnapped—my foster brother. I understand wanting to protect yourself, but if you have any information—"

"Look, some of my clients talk. Mostly about themselves, to brag to me, but no one is dumb enough to tell me about a kidnapping."

"Not even Senator Silva?" He watched her reaction, knowing he was taking a risk by revealing what he knew. But he had to go for it. Time was running out.

She blinked in surprise. "Henry?" Then she giggled, the action so out of character for the polished woman that he believed her reaction. "Oh, honey, he's pretty to look at and has a great dick, but he's a moron." Wiping away a stray tear of laughter she stood, her whole body still shaking with true humor. "He didn't kidnap anyone."

"What about Adam Berch?"

She paused, then nodded slowly. "I mean, sure, I wouldn't put anything past him. But I don't like the man—he's not allowed inside here. Not that he comes with Henry anymore. Not even to wait in his SUV down the street. The man is a shark with a mean streak, that much I know. So, yes, I could see him kidnapping someone. But not Henry."

"I expect that our conversation—"

"Will remain between us. I won't say a word to Henry. And if you ever do change your mind, for real, I'll always keep a spot open for you." She winked, her expression sly. "And your friend. She's stunning, and I love a woman with fire."

"I'll relay the message to her."

"Please do." She leaned in for another hug, which he obliged, then he hurried after Reese.

He found her waiting half a block down, her expression dry.

"Did she buy my outraged act?"

He grinned. "Enough that I was able to plant a listening device under the drink tray."

"I got one under the coffee table when I was pointing my finger in her face so we'll see if she notices."

"She probably sweeps for devices periodically."

"Let's just hope she concentrates her searches in the bedroom area." Because they needed a lead—anything to find Easton.

CHAPTER 25

—When life gives you lemons, it's time to open the gin.—

"Would you stop fidgeting?" Jesse took Hailey's hand in his as their driver pulled under the porte cochere of the historic building.

The exclusive event cost twenty thousand a person, had a celebrity auction, and was invite-only. Thankfully, there was no theme for this one as was the case with some galas he was invited to. It was simply formal dress required.

"This dress is too tight," she grumbled.

"The dress is perfect, and so are you." He tangled his fingers with hers as he drank in the sight of her again. The car line was long, so he took advantage of this time alone with her.

The dress she'd settled on was a plain black with a high boat-neck cut covered in a mesh lace. The back dipped low—too low according to her—and also featured a mesh lace insert. All her skin was exposed but still somehow concealed, making him want to touch her everywhere. Though to be fair, he always wanted to do that.

"You can't say stuff like that."

"I can if it's true."

"Well, you're not the one *not* wearing any underwear."

The driver from the front snickered before clearing his throat.

"I can take mine off if it'll make you feel better."

"You guys remember that I can hear you, right?" Elijah's voice came through the imperceptible earpieces they both wore.

Jesse hadn't forgotten exactly, but he hadn't been thinking about the other man once Hailey started talking about her underwear.

Or lack of them.

Hailey simply gave Jesse a dry look, but whatever she was about to say was cut off when someone opened their door.

Jesse slid out first, ignoring the valet who offered to take Hailey's hand. Instead, he blocked her with his body, not wanting anyone to get a picture of her stepping out. Then he slid an arm around her shoulders and ushered her toward the front doors of the museum, ignoring the handful of photographers standing behind the velvet ropes.

"Mr. Lennox, let us get a picture!"

"Who's your date?"

He kept walking.

"Yikes, is it like this for you all the time?" she murmured as they stepped inside, handing her wrap over to the coat check.

"No, definitely not, but I wasn't expected to be here." He took the coat check stub and tucked it into his pocket before he slid his hand right back into hers. "You ready for tonight?"

"Yep. I'm keeping this dress, by the way." Her voice was low as she smiled up at him.

A flash caught his attention, and he realized there were photographers inside. He'd hoped to dodge them for the most part, but unfortunately some things were unavoidable. "I thought you hated it."

"Sure, but I look good in it."

He grinned back at her. "You're ridiculous."

"True. So...did you ever expect to end up here?" She glanced around the open museum, where high-top tables had been set up between some of the displays. They were all covered with thick black tablecloths and topped with glittering gold centerpieces.

Servers milled about carrying appetizer trays and flutes of champagne. Luckily this wasn't a sit-down event, but more of a mingling one. The kind he preferred, if he had to choose. Though he hated them all for the most part. At one end of the huge room, a stage had been set up for the celebrity auction, and the individual silent auctions were arranged on tables around the room.

"No, not really." He steered her toward one of the silent auction tables. "I just always wanted to create, to make the world better. Some things that have come with making money are startling. It's... a different world than I ever expected," he said honestly. "Luckily, I had a rich roommate my first year in college who quite literally explained to me a lot of things I didn't understand."

Like how the wealthy summered in certain places, or how much of a difference generational wealth made in giving a lot of the kids he'd gone to school with a leg up in life. It helped them in a way Jesse was certain they'd never truly understand. They'd all had these lifelong connections with each other. Not to mention nepotism that landed so many of them jobs after college. Or internships. Just so many opportunities a lot of them took for granted.

She looked up at him in surprise.

"What?"

"I just never thought about it like that. That you were thrown into a whole new world after..." She cleared her throat. "I'm glad you found good people to help you along the way."

"I did." There had also been a lot of rich pricks he'd had to deal with in the early years, like his second-year roommate who'd thought it was hilarious that Jesse had needed a job to pay for extras (like *food*). Last he'd heard, that guy had dropped out his senior year after a scandal and was currently in rehab for who knew what.

"I wish I'd been there for you." Hailey's words were quiet, sincere, and they startled him as he slid a bid card into the auction box—for a trip for two to Paris. Whether he won or not, he planned to take Hailey there. And anywhere else she wanted to go.

He didn't get a chance to respond because Ian Warren approached him, a smile on his smarmy face.

"Jesse!" His voice was annoyingly booming.

But Jesse kept a neutral expression as the lawyer approached. This was better than he'd hoped, because he'd thought they'd have to search for the man. "Ian, nice to see you."

Ian pumped his hand a couple times, squeezing way too hard, and, whew, Jesse could smell the whiskey wafting off him. This event had just started, but apparently the man was going to tie one on.

"You too. It's a wonderful surprise that you're here. And who is this lovely lady?"

"Ian Warren, this is Hailey West."

Hailey smiled at the man politely and snagged a glass of champagne off the tray of a passing server.

"I hear you called my office today. I'm sorry I didn't get a chance to return it."

"No problem at all." He glanced around, pretending to be bored and disinterested. Because that was the way to hook a man like Ian Warren.

"Would you two excuse me?" Hailey murmured, looking just as bored. "I see someone I need to speak to."

"Of course," Ian responded before Jesse could.

Hailey smiled at the man, passing by him closely. And even though Jesse was watching, he couldn't see if she'd stolen the man's cell phone or not.

Until he heard her whisper, "Got it," over the earpiece.

"So what can I help you with?"

Jesse could practically see the dollar signs in the other man's eyes. He glanced around again, this time acting as if he needed privacy. "Your firm has a good reputation for prenups and other marriage-related things. I was hoping to set up an appointment to talk about that."

Warren's eyes widened in surprise, probably for a couple reasons. The whole marriage talk being one, considering Jesse had never been linked to anyone publicly. And two, it was common enough knowledge that he had attorneys he was happy with.

"I'm not looking to change firms," Jesse added. "Rather I'm looking to work with another firm specifically for this only. And I want a specialist."

"Ah, I see. So is your date…" He trailed off, glancing in the direction Hailey had gone.

Jesse simply nodded. "We've known each other a long time."

"Who is she? What does she do? If you don't mind my asking. It's just that I've never seen you bring anyone to these things."

He gave a small smile. "She hates these events, so I very rarely ask her to attend. And she's in cybersecurity," was all he said, giving the attorney a look. The man could interpret that however he chose—he would assume that Hailey was involved in one of the three-letter agencies as a spook of sorts. Which wasn't too far off from the truth.

"Ah." The man nodded conspiratorially. "So we'll want to cover all your assets, future children if you plan to have any—"

Laughing lightly, Jesse nodded. "Absolutely, but I think it's a bit too much to talk about when I haven't even proposed," he murmured. "I'd like to set up a meeting with you in the next week before we make things official."

"Of course, of course. By the way, I'm sorry to hear about what happened at FACE, Inc. What happened exactly?"

People milled around them as the place started to fill up, the voices growing louder. "Honestly we're not sure yet, but the FBI has things under control. Thankfully, no one was injured."

"Good, good," he said, nodding profusely. "Terrible times we're living in. Do they think it's terrorism or…"

Jesse gave a mournful look as he shook his head. "They're not telling me anything. I trust them to figure things out, but I am frustrated with the opacity of the investigation. Even if I understand it," he tacked on.

"Of course, of course." Warren nodded again, but perked up easily as Hailey approached them, a new glass of champagne in her hand, her smile wide.

The man looked her over like she was a piece of meat, and it took all Jesse's control to keep his expression neutral.

"So what have you boys been chatting about?" she asked teasingly as she slid up next to Jesse, wrapped her arm around his middle.

"How lucky we are to have such better halves."

Warren's laugh was booming as he nodded in agreement. "Too true."

Hailey squeezed Jesse's side letting him know everything was done.

Before the man could continue the conversation, Jesse held out his hand. "It was good to see you. I'll call you next week and set that thing up."

Warren nodded, his smile firmly in place as Jesse and Hailey made their way down the row of auction tables.

"We're good?"

"Yep." She grinned up at him, then her smile fell a fraction.

"What is it?"

She glanced down at the latest table, an auction for a spa weekend at a place in New Hampshire. "Just feels weird to be here at all when Easton is..." Jaw clenched, she shook her head before she pasted on a smile.

"We're here for him."

"I know that. Every fiber of me knows that. I just...I wish this was over. I wish we had him safe. I've been fighting my emotions, and apparently now they've decided to bubble up and—"

Leaning down, he brushed his lips over hers, kissing her gently, then not so gently, before he pulled back. "We're going to find him," he growled softly.

"This is gold," Elijah said, his voice cutting through their earpieces, bringing both of them back to reality. "Good job, Hailey."

"I didn't even see you take or return it." Jesse kept his voice low as they drifted into the crowd, then turned to avoid someone he didn't want to talk to.

"I've got magic hands," she murmured.

"Don't I know it."

"Still here, guys," Elijah grumbled.

Hailey grinned up at Jesse and didn't respond to Elijah. "Let's continue making the rounds. Have you seen the others yet?"

"They just arrived," Elijah said. He'd put them on different frequencies, but if necessary, could patch them all in together.

Something Jesse was glad for. Having to focus on multiple conversations in his ear while talking to people right in front of him sounded like a nightmare.

At least they were one step closer to finding Easton. Or he hoped they were. And he hoped that Cash and Reese had just as much luck as they had. Or better.

"The senator just arrived as well, per Cash," Elijah said.

"What's he driving?" Hailey asked as a couple Jesse vaguely recognized approached them.

"The newest G-wagon. Obsidian black." Then he rattled off the license plate.

"Thanks," she whispered before pasting on a smile to greet the newcomers.

CHAPTER 26

—At some point it's okay to accept that some people are just assholes.—

"Constantine, it's such a pleasure to see you here. What a delightful surprise." Alice Silva—the senator's wife—air-kissed him, her smile as big as her Botox allowed, he guessed.

Cash was aware of Reese side-eyeing him at the "Constantine" because, yep, that was his name. But his friends called him Cash. Always had. "It's a pleasure to see you too. Alice, this is Reese Sinclair, my date for the evening."

When Alice looked at Reese, her smile was as fake as usual, but then she blinked. "Reese, you're Eleanor and Archibald's daughter?"

"Yes." Reese's smile was tight.

So, of course, Cash was now curious about them.

"Oh, I wish they were here tonight. Your father loves to brag about you. You're in cybersecurity, correct?"

Reese looked a little stunned at the brag comment, but she recovered quickly. "That's correct. I've been following the work you've done at the KIDS' TOMORROW literacy foundation, and it's incredible." She smoothly shifted topics, and even though she'd told Cash she couldn't stand the woman or her husband because of their politics, he'd have never guessed.

"Thank you. It's a project of my heart. Something your date knows," she said on a laugh, looking at Cash now. "Thank you again for the generous donation. With the extra building, we've got a lot more space now for tutoring and mentoring." She held her hand out and squeezed his, her expression sincere for the first time tonight.

"You donated a building?" Reese asked.

"Oh, he did more than that, he donated books and—"

He cleared his throat, laughing. "I did what I could. That's all."

"You're too humble," she said, squeezing his upper arm. "I wish more men were like you."

"Constantine!" The senator joined them, and it was subtle, but Cash saw the tightening around Alice's eyes, even though her smile remained in place. "She's right, you know. I'm so glad you're here tonight, and I was hoping to talk to you about something." He shook Cash's hand, completely dismissing Reese—and even his wife.

And the only reason Cash went along was because now was his chance to attempt to clone the man's phone. "Sure, no problem."

"We're good. You boys go talk," Alice said, her laugh brittle and nothing like earlier as she turned back to talk to Reese.

"What can I help you with?" Cash asked, stepping away—and hating to be separated from Reese.

"I heard you're bidding on the Stapleton project."

That was what he wanted to talk about?

"Ah, my company is, yes." A company he'd started from the ground up, but he was now looking for a new challenge. Some days he wondered if something was wrong with him because he couldn't simply be satisfied. He'd earned his nickname of Cash because everything he touched allegedly turned to cash. Maybe the name had a better ring than gold.

"I've got a couple suggestions for contractors." The man droned on about two contractors he wanted to recommend—both known for shoddy work.

"Get him to pull his phone out," Elijah said in his ear.

He was trying to find a moment to interrupt and do just that. It would be easier if Cash could actually swipe the senator's phone as Hailey planned to do with that shady lawyer, but that wasn't Cash's skill set. And Elijah had the capability to clone as long as they were close enough and the man's phone was unlocked. "Hey, would you mind texting me the names of the contractors? I plan on enjoying myself tonight and don't want to forget."

"Of course, but I don't have my phone on me. Never bring them to these things. I won't forget though. Tell you what, I'll email you in the morning."

"Great." *Absolutely fantastic.* But he pasted on a smile as the other man continued droning on. Jesus, he liked the sound of his own voice.

***

"You look like you need a drink," Reese murmured as Cash approached.

What he needed was some Reese, but he kept that thought to himself. "Well, that was a bust." And he hated the feeling of wasting time, especially with Easton's life in the balance.

"Maybe not." Reese smiled as she slid her arm through his. "I cloned Alice's phone. Which might give us nothing, but it's better than nothing at all."

He glanced down at her in surprise. "How'd you do that?"

"She asked for my phone number, and when she unlocked her phone I took advantage." She shrugged, but looked very pleased with herself. Her dark hair was up in a twist, showing off her delicate neck, and he wanted to lean down and pepper kisses along all that smooth, exposed skin.

Since that was likely to get him slapped, he ignored the impulse. "Any sign of Berch?" he murmured as they slowly made their way through the crowd. He recognized a lot of faces, some simply from television.

"No, not that I expected it." Her voice was just as low, and with the din of voices and the live band playing, no one could overhear them anyway. "So, *Constantine,* you donated a building?"

Technically he'd donated a building, then completed the construction of another one, eating all the costs. "It's a good tax write-off."

She gave him a dry look.

Which made him grin. "So, your parents live in DC and know Alice Silva?" He figured it was a fair question if she was calling him Constantine.

To his surprise, her expression shuttered. "They split their time between here and New York. They're lobbyists. I didn't even realize they knew her, but I shouldn't be surprised. They know everyone."

Oh, there was definitely more there, but he didn't push. He was playing the long game with this woman, though it was no game at all.

"I'm patching Hailey in," Elijah's voice sounded in his ear, reminding him that the other man was listening.

Because he'd actually forgotten for a moment.

"It's me," Hailey said a second later in his earpiece. "We did what we needed to do, and we're getting out of here. Target One is leaving so we're going to follow."

Target One referred to the senator. "Sounds good," Cash said as they reached the valet under the porte cochere. "I'm sure you know how we fared by now too."

"Yep. We've got our phones if you need us." He heard the subtle click letting him know that she'd ended the connection.

"So what do you want to do?" Reese asked as she looked up at him.

"Cash, darling!" A familiar voice rang out, making him wince.

Isabella Vance.

The tall redhead approached, a calculating smile in place as she air-kissed Cash, completely ignoring Reese—who was trying to ease away from him.

So he slid an arm around Reese's shoulders and pulled her close as he stepped back from Isabella, avoiding what looked like a potential hug. He didn't want the woman touching him.

"You're leaving already?" she asked before he'd said a word.

"Yep." He kept his arm securely in place around Reese's shoulders and decided not to ask any questions or invite conversation. It made things awkward, but he was petty enough not to give a shit at the moment.

"Oh, that's too bad." She pouted a little, then finally looked at Reese, her smile firmly in place. "I'm Isabella."

"I'm Reese." She nodded politely but didn't offer her hand or anything.

For the first time since Cash had known her, Isabella seemed flustered. "Well...it's good to see you. I'll reach out, and we can set up lunch." Then she hurried inside as the valet finally pulled up with his vehicle.

"I didn't think you could pull off the icy thing, but you did that well," Reese said once they were alone in his SUV and heading out.

He lifted a shoulder.

"So is she an ex? Because I know who she is, and she's engaged to that, uh, that guy who looks like a Kennedy but isn't, right?"

"Yep."

"Is that all I'm gonna get?" Reese shifted slightly, crossing one leg over the other as she started pulling pins from her hair.

He tried not to stare at the swath of smooth skin as her dress split over her crossed legs, the fabric falling on either side of them. She wasn't paying attention either, wasn't trying to be coy or whatever as she grumbled about all the "dumb pins" in her hair.

"If you tell me about your parents, I'll tell you about Isabella."

Now he got the grumpy look he was getting used to from her. "Fine, whatever. We'll both keep our secrets." Before she could continue, his phone buzzed with an incoming text.

"Open it for me?" he asked, giving her his code.

"Oh, hell, it's Chloe. She attached a picture of the listening devices we planted with an angry face emoji. But she also says to come over, she has something for us."

"Could be a trap."

"Are you armed?" Reese asked.

"Always."

"Then we're good. Let's go." She slid her dress up higher to reveal a blade strapped to her thigh. "Because I'm armed too."

He swerved slightly at the sight of her lifting her dress and showing off a weapon. Why was that so hot? Okay, he knew why. "How'd you get that through security earlier tonight?"

"It's not metal, doesn't set anything off." She gave a casual shrug, and he forced his gaze back to the road ahead.

Because the urge to look at her, to simply drink her in, was going to cause him to crash if he wasn't careful.

The rest of the drive was quiet enough, with the city bright around them until he turned into the established neighborhood where Chloe Grace lived. He wondered if her neighbors knew what she did for a living, doubted they cared. Because Chloe would be discreet, and hell, maybe some of her neighbors were her clients, considering the amount of wealth in this zip code.

Thankfully, he found parking close by so Reese wouldn't have to hoof it far in her heels. Not that she was complaining, but he didn't want her to have to.

As they reached the top of the steps to the brownstone, the front door opened up. Chloe wore soft-looking, wide-legged pants, a fuzzy sweater, and her face was completely made-up. So maybe she was expecting company. Her expression was neutral as she stepped back to let them in, but as they entered the foyer, she said, "You don't go any farther into my house after what you pulled."

"It's not personal," Reese said before he could. "We're looking for someone, and we'll cross a lot of lines to find him."

Chloe's expression was tight as she glanced between the two of them. She handed them the smashed devices, then sighed. "Look, I don't like having enemies. And you're one of the most decent humans I know, so... Henry has been talking about hitting it big soon. Nothing too specific. He likes to talk, and he loves to brag about his accomplishments. And I'm using that phrase lightly, because like I said...he's just not that bright. But he's betting a lot of his money on some big pharma thing, thinking it's going to make him 'Midas rich' by the end of next year. I don't know any more than that, and I definitely don't know anything about a kidnapping—which I still don't think he's smart enough to pull off. I know what I do is technically illegal, but it shouldn't be. And other than that, I walk the straight and narrow, whether you believe me or not. So if this isn't enough for you, then I guess we're enemies."

"We're not enemies," Cash said softly, believing her. He felt like a bit of a dick for planting those devices, but Reese hadn't been wrong. He would break a lot of laws to find Easton. "And for the record, I'm sorry about hiding these." He'd shoved the broken pieces into the pocket of his tux.

Chloe shoved out a breath, nodded once. "Okay, then." She looked between the two of them again. "I hope you find your friend."

"Thank you," he said, meaning it.

Reese didn't say anything at all, simply nodded and headed out, Cash right behind her. "Do you believe her?" she asked once they were alone in his vehicle.

"I do. She seemed sincere, and I'm guessing she already weighed the pros and cons of making an enemy of me. And by extension, Jesse as well."

Reese simply nodded, clearly lost in thought as she turned to look out the window as he headed back to Jesse's place. What he wouldn't give to know what she was thinking. Hell, what he wouldn't give if she'd give him a chance.

CHapTer 27

—A negative mind will never give you a positive life.—

When she saw Reese's name on her caller ID, Hailey answered on the first ring. "Hey, we're en route to the senator's house. The tracker I planted on his vehicle just stopped there." And though she doubted the man would be leaving for the rest of the night, they were still going to stake out his place for a while. She'd rather be close to the guy if he made a move.

"We're headed back to Jesse's, but the night wasn't a total bust at least." Reese quickly recapped what she and Cash had learned from Chloe, then said, "I'll be monitoring Warren's phone as well as Alice Silva's all night. Elijah and I agreed to give each other breaks."

"We'll monitor Alice Silva's for now during the stakeout, so don't worry about her for the next few hours… But I think we might need to ask for help soon. I was thinking of pulling in one of the guys to help monitor everything." Because she didn't want to miss something.

"Okay, sounds good. I've got my phone if you need me."

Almost as soon as Reese hung up, Hailey received a text from her.

We ran into a woman at the gala named Isabella. I think she's one of Cash's exes. Do you know if Cash dated her?

Well, since Hailey hadn't been in contact with Cash over the years other than the letters he'd sent her, *no*. And she hated the reminder of that.

No, want me to ask Jesse about her? she texted back.

NO was the only response.

Okay, then.

"Everything good?" Jesse asked as he looked over at the gated house across the street. It was a few houses down from where they were parked, but they had a good view of the end of the driveway.

"Yeah, I think so. Did Special Agent Parker call you again?"

"No, maybe he's given up."

She snorted softly as she looked down at her laptop and turned up the volume of the app they used for any phones they cloned during investigations. Since they were parked in a nice neighborhood after dark, she tilted the face of the laptop down so the light wasn't a bright beacon to any potential neighbors watching. She'd already put it on a darker mode but wanted to be careful. "We might have to drive somewhere else and park. There's a good chance we're going to get the cops called on us. I just hate to go too far…" She trailed off as a voice came through her computer.

Alice Silva.

Hailey eased the lid open and maximized the app to full screen. The number Silva had called showed up as private, which was unusual. Hailey should have been able to see it.

"Henry won't be back for hours," Alice said, her tone dry. "He made up some stupid excuse about getting drinks after the gala, but he's going to be with one of his whores."

Male laughter followed, but no audible response.

"So get over here and fuck me before he gets back. We can do it in his bed." Her tone was breathy. "I'll turn off the cameras, but park down the street."

"Give me twenty." Then the man disconnected.

"You recognize the voice?" Hailey asked, looking at Jesse.

He shook his head. "No."

"So if the senator isn't here, then Alice took his vehicle after the gala. Which means he has another mode of transportation."

"He likely just called a private car service," Jesse said. "The man probably has an account with them under a pseudonym for this very reason."

She blinked at him in surprise. "Seriously?"

Jesse nodded, his expression dry. "It's common enough among his subset of assholes. That way there's no tracking his movements via his vehicle's GPS. And he probably turns his phone off or leaves it at home. Obviously not everyone is that smart, or we'd never have public scandals, but yes, this is a known modus operandi for some cheaters in DC."

"Jesus," she muttered. "Well, he did tell you that he left his phone at home."

"Want to stay and see who shows up?"

She nodded. "Hell, yeah. Might come in handy to find out who the senator's wife is screwing." Although now she felt like they were not necessarily back at square one, but... Hailey wanted to punch something. "I can't believe it's only been a few days since he was taken," she muttered. Because it felt like an entire lifetime.

"I know." Jesse reached out and took her hand in his, squeezed once. She saw the guilt in his eyes and squeezed back.

"Stop beating yourself up. I can see you doing it."

He looked away, but didn't drop her hand. "I should have been there with him," he finally said.

"By that logic, I should have too. It's my fault way more than yours. You've been there for him for years." And she'd disappeared like a coward. "And if I'm being totally transparent... I was supposed to meet Easton for lunch too. I think he must have been trying to get us all together again."

Sneaky, sneaky man. One she desperately wanted to find.

Jesse blinked in true surprise, then his lips curved up wryly. "Easton really is sneaky." His words mirrored her thoughts.

When her phone buzzed, she pulled her hand away to open up the incoming text. It was from Hazel.

Any idea where Adam Berch is?

No, Hailey texted back. *No luck on your end?* Well, duh, she thought after she'd sent the text. Otherwise, Hazel wouldn't have texted her.

You better not be lying to me.

I'm not! And why the hell would Hazel say that?

We've got a contact who saw you and Jesse talking to the senator tonight at the gala and Berch works for him.

Yeah, no shit. *Why do you think we were there? We were fishing for information!*

There was a veeerrrry long pause. Then, *We're currently working on getting a warrant to tap the senator's phones because of his relationship with Berch. Haven't pulled him in yet because we know we'll tip our hand and then he'll lawyer up. And this information is not for public consumption.*

It wasn't like she needed the disclaimer. Ignoring the last bit, she texted back: *You think the senator is involved?*

Berch works for the senator. If he paid Beeker to blow up that lab, someone paid HIM to do it. He's a hired gun, nothing more. It stands to reason the senator is involved. We just can't figure out why. What did you find out tonight?

Ah, so this was a fishing expedition on Hazel's part. *Not much, unfortunately.* Hailey paused, then decided to tell her what Reese and Cash had found out. *The senator is looking to cash in on some big payday. Something to do with Innovative Labs. No other details than that, but he's up to something. Not sure if it has anything to do with Easton's kidnapping.* Though her gut told her the two things had to be connected, especially considering Easton's area of expertise and the fact that all his research had been destroyed. At least the physical aspects of it.

Keep me updated.

I will. So why hasn't Special Agent Parker come after Jesse and me? Jesse had literally kicked in Beeker's door and interrogated him—and they were caught on security cameras. That was the definition of impeding an investigation.

I convinced him not to. If he brings either of you in, especially Jesse, it'll make the news and tip off Berch and anyone else that you're involved.

Okay, then. *Thx. I owe you.*

Yeah you do, and I will collect.

"We don't need to worry about the Feds at the moment," Hailey said as she set her phone down. "Hazel convinced Parker to leave us out of this for now."

"Good," he murmured, seemingly unfazed regardless, his gaze trained across the street. "I see movement."

She followed his line of sight and saw a hooded man walking down the sidewalk before quickly turning into the open gates of the Silva mansion. "Let's wait a few minutes, then drive around, see if we can find his car parked." Shouldn't be too hard to run the license plate of Alice Silva's lover.

Not that Hailey really thought this would matter, but information was power and could help them in the long run. Hell, maybe not even with this job, but another one. Not that Hailey thought of this as a job. This was a fight for Easton's life.

After five minutes passed, Jesse started up his SUV, and they slowly cruised down the quiet street. "Do you like living in the DC/Virginia area?" she asked as he made a left when the street T-boned. She'd been wondering.

For reasons.

"Ah...check it out," he said instead of responding, nodding at a solo vehicle parked along the curb.

It was a Mercedes sedan, neutral gray color, dark window tint, but not too dark. Didn't stand out in this neighborhood, with the exception that there weren't any other vehicles parked on the street. Everyone else had their vehicles tucked in nicely in their heated garages.

She snapped a picture of the license plate as Jesse cruised by, then plugged it into the system one of the founders of Redemption Harbor Consulting and now Security, Gage Yates, had created, then refined years ago. And... "Oh shit, this license plate doesn't exist."

Jesse frowned at her. "What?"

"It usually means that someone cut apart two different license plates, then welded two together. It's pretty standard among a certain subset of thieves. Can you kill the lights and pull up to the vehicle? I'm going to plant a tracker because whoever this is, is more interesting than I originally thought."

Clearly, Alice Silva was screwing someone with a certain set of skills.

Jesse glanced around, obviously not liking it, but he killed the lights and parked a few houses away from the solo vehicle.

Hailey moved fast, glad they'd had the foresight to bring a change of clothes. Moving in her black pants and sweater was a lot easier than working in the gown from earlier. She stretched out on the pavement and crawled under the Mercedes instead of just planting it in an easily accessible spot. She wanted to make sure this thing was hidden.

As she scooted farther under the car, she heard a vehicle drive past her, realized it was Jesse. *What the hell?*

Aaannnd that was when she heard footsteps along the sidewalk. *Oh crap.* Heart racing, she pulled her feet up so that they weren't visible to anyone walking by.

But that was when she heard the *beep beep* of the car above her.

Craaaap.

As she tensed, trying to decide what to do, the passenger door opened up.

She froze. Well, *stayed* frozen as she turned to look at heavily booted feet as someone leaned into the vehicle, softly whistling to themselves. There was a slight rummaging sound.

A moment later, the guy stepped back onto the curb, his feet disappearing from sight as the door slammed. She waited for something, anything, then heard the bootsteps thudding away in the direction they'd come. She didn't move right away, but stayed quiet for another minute to make sure the guy was really gone.

Breathing hard, she secured the tracking device and slid out from the back of the vehicle.

Jesse was already there, and she almost yelped, but he grabbed her hand and pulled her to her feet. And that was when she saw the weapon in his hand.

But he held a finger to his lips, then motioned to where he'd parked in someone's driveway.

Heart still an erratic tattoo in her chest, she hurried with him to the waiting vehicle. Once she slid into the passenger seat, she said, "Holy shit, that was cl—"

Jesse practically lunged at her, claiming her mouth in a heated kiss as he consumed her. When he finally pulled back, they were both breathing hard.

"You're never doing anything like that again," he growled.

She blinked as he started the engine, his movements jerky as he pulled out of the parking spot. "It wasn't a big deal... Besides, I've been in way worse situations."

Oh, that wasn't the right thing to say.

"Well, you won't be ever again."

"Jesse—"

"Nope. Just no. I don't want to hear it." He let out a savage curse, then looked in the rearview mirror as he continued down the street. "I think he came back for condoms or something."

"Did you get a good look at his face?"

"No. I parked in that driveway hoping he'd think I lived there. Then I snuck out the passenger side and used the shadows to double back. If he'd seen you..." He shook his head, not finishing what she knew he'd planned to say.

That Jesse would have used the pistol if needed.

"That was really smart," she said instead of the thoughts ricocheting around in her brain.

He was silent for a long moment, then said, "I don't like that this is part of your everyday job."

"Well, it's not really. I'm usually the one running a job, doing the behind-the-scenes techy stuff and making sure everyone else stays in their lane. Occasionally, I do engage in stakeouts and on-the-ground stuff—we're all trained the same—but I'm not normally rolling around under cars planting trackers."

He shot her a sideways look. "For some reason, I don't believe you."

"I swear." *Mostly.* She bit back the last word, however, as he steered them home.

No, not home, to his place. Something she needed to remember. Because when this was all over, she'd be leaving.

CHAPTER 28

Easton sat back in the chair across from a man who was calling himself John. If Easton was into gambling, he'd bet everything that wasn't the dark-haired man's name.

"Just tell us what you need, and we'll get it for you. We want to work together as a team." The man's voice was a little raspy, but oddly soothing.

Which was just an illusion. "So are you the good cop, then? Or good kidnapper, whatever."

The man's eyes narrowed a fraction, but then that easy smile was back in place. "My associates got a little carried away at first, didn't understand how important you are."

Uh-huh. Yeah, right. Easton kept his expression as neutral as possible. He'd been drugged again, then moved to some sort of lab. Everything here was state of the art, a lot different than the cold, empty house he'd been in before. He looked around the room again, though he'd already memorized most of the items in it. Whoever had kitted this place out had some serious money.

"Just tell me what you want, and we can move forward from there." They'd released his wrist and ankle restraints as well, so he had range of movement.

But the guy in front of him, while acting all concerned, was definitely trained. And armed. His gun was hidden, but Easton had seen the bulge at his back earlier when he'd turned to talk to the other armed guy by the door. Now, that guy wasn't hiding his weapons. As in plural.

"I know you've been working on new treatments for ALS."

Easton blinked, nodded. "Yeah." It wasn't a secret—he'd published articles about it and had been featured in a few online journals.

"I've also heard that you're close to finding a cure."

Well, that was a big fat lie. But Easton wanted to live, so he nodded slowly, acting as if he was weighing telling the truth or not. "You have good sources."

Apparently, it was the right thing to say because the guy's mouth curved up slightly. "We blew up your lab."

Wait…what? Easton blinked, tried to digest the words. "Was anyone hurt?" he managed to rasp out through his surprise. His coworkers, friends… Oh wait, Jesse.

"No, of course not." The man dismissed his question. "But all your research has been destroyed. And you're going to replicate it."

He frowned at the man. "All my research is online. In the cloud."

The man gave a patient nod. "Yes, we figured as much. You're going to log into your account with FACE, Inc. and download all your research. And you'll be monitored the entire time."

"That's all you want? Why did you go to all the trouble of kidnapping me, then?"

"Because of how close you are to finding a cure—and we haven't been able to hack into your files."

If he gave them all his files, he'd be useless to them. They'd kill him. Well, he was certain they'd kill him eventually anyway. Because none of them had been wearing masks. He'd thought maybe he'd been kidnapped because of the suspected money laundering he'd stumbled onto. A colleague from Innovative Labs had come to him about an issue with odd financials and labs that didn't seem to exist, so Easton had started looking into it in his spare time as a favor. But his own research was in a different stratosphere of what he'd imagined he'd been taken for.

"You'll have anything you need at your disposal. You just have to ask. How close do you think you are?"

He rubbed a hand over his face, trying to ground himself. Because he had to think fast, to lie his ass off. Something he hated to do. But to stay alive, he'd do it. "A few weeks out, maybe a couple months. If you really did blow up my lab, I'll need to replicate some experiments, but mostly all my and my team's research is saved."

The man nodded, clearly pleased—and clearly a dumbass. "Good, we'll get started, then."

He nodded once at the guard, who opened the door, stepped out, then returned with a laptop.

After "John" set it in front of him, he sat right next to him. "Get all the information you need."

Easton was stiff as he worked, his fingers flying over the keyboard as he logged into his Cloud account. "These are the files," he said, nodding at the screen. "This is a lot of information. Can this laptop handle it if I transfer?"

The man simply nodded so Easton got to work transferring. It took a while, but once he was done, the man said, "That's it?"

Easton nodded, wondering if this was when he was going to die. Sure, he could have refused to grab all his research, but then he'd have been tortured or killed. And he needed to buy himself time, to figure out a way from wherever here was. Besides, it was clear they needed him to work on this anyway because there weren't any other scientists here. And he'd have to do more live trials...something these people didn't seem to understand.

The man slid the laptop away from Easton, then plugged in a red flash drive. Easton watched as something started happening to his Cloud account.

All the information started to disappear, as if it was being eaten up by bugs.

"What are you doing?" he demanded.

"Corrupting your account." Looking pleased with himself, the man stood, laptop in hand. "I'll be back shortly." His tone was dismissive as he left the room, watching the destruction on-screen.

Nausea swelled up inside Easton as he thought of all his work being destroyed. He had other backups, but this was the most comprehensive of all of his research over the years. He jolted to his feet, and the guard shoved off the door, but he ignored the man as he bent over a nearby stainless-steel garbage can and threw up, emptying what little contents remained of the food they'd recently fed him.

He really needed to get out of here.

CHAPTer 29

Six years ago

Dear Cash,

I'm writing another letter I'll never send you. I asked around (aka called in some favors), and it sounds like you're doing well. Not that I'm surprised. I hope you've found what you're looking for.

I also heard that you're into some sort of "illegal" smuggling of vodka and other things that sound like they're right up your alley. Hope you're watching your six. I miss you.

Sincerely,

Assface

***

Dear Easton,

I keep trying to work up the courage to call you, then keep chickening out. So I write letters I know I'll never send. I've read a few articles about your recent research and can't help but feel so proud that I knew you "before." You're amazing, and I hope you know that. I mean, I'm sure you do, considering all you've accomplished at such a young age, but it bears saying more than once.

You are amazing, and hopefully one day I'll manage to get over my bullshit. It just feels like so much time has passed, and I think...what if you guys don't care anymore?

Love,

Hailey

***

Dear Jesse,

I've never stopped thinking about you, never stopped dreaming about "what if," and I've never stopped loving you. I reread all your letters to the point they're crumpled and thin. Some of the guys give me shit for it and are always asking about the letters, but they're just for me. I do share all the other stuff the three of you send. I think the Christmas tree is still the favorite, even years later. It even made it stateside and is now in the barracks in a designated corner. We all add random decorations to it. Mostly penis related. Guys are way too obsessed with penises. And...I'm going to stop there.

Always yours,

Hailey

CHAPTER 30

—I do this thing called "exactly what I want."—

Jesse kept his arm wrapped around Hailey as he spooned her from behind. They'd arrived back at his place a few hours ago and crashed. She was still sleeping, but he'd woken up half an hour ago and couldn't go back to sleep. Too much was on his mind.

Things he shouldn't be worrying about at all.

Like his future with Hailey.

It was about five now, but the sun wasn't up yet. Something had changed between them last night. He'd felt it in the air right after she'd planted that tracker and he'd kissed her like he was dying. Because he'd felt as if he had been. When that hooded man had walked up to the Mercedes, Jesse had felt his finger twitch on the trigger of his pistol, and that terrified him.

That loss of control and sense.

But if that man had proven to be a threat, Jesse knew he'd have done what needed to be done. After they'd left, however, Hailey had retreated into herself. And he wasn't certain why.

Yeah, they'd still had sex when they'd gotten back, and he'd done everything he could to imprint himself on her, but she was keeping something from him. Or keeping walls up.

Maybe both.

He'd thought... Who knew what he'd thought? Clearly, he still didn't under-stand the naked woman curled up against him. Maybe he never had. But he knew one thing: He wanted about a hundred thousand more years to learn everything about her.

And that still wouldn't be enough.

He nibbled her earlobe, his cock impatient, and—

His bedroom door flew open. Cash, fully dressed, didn't bat an eye at the two of them together. "Easton, or someone with his password, logged into his Cloud account."

Hailey shoved up with him, clutching the sheet over her breasts. "What?"

"Reese has been monitoring it since you gave her the password and—"

"Yeah, I know. So he logged in?"

"Hopefully, it was him," Cash said. "And Reese says someone tried to insert a virus, but it didn't work. Wants you to look at it."

If Easton hadn't logged in, then someone had hacked his account—doubt-ful—or someone had tortured the information out of him. That thought, well, he couldn't go there. *Nope.*

"Get out of here unless you want to see my ass," Hailey said, already throwing the covers off.

Cash turned quickly, slamming the door shut behind him as she scrambled for her clothes.

"We should be able to track the IP of wherever Easton logged in. If he's still in the area..." Hailey paused as she pulled a dark T-shirt on over a black sports bra with a picture of skeleton hands cupping her breasts—she was still wonderfully weird even in little ways and... he'd missed her. "I don't know what we'll be walking into. I'm going to call my boss, see if we can get some backup."

Jesse was moving as well, pulling on clothes. "I'll let my security know we'll be heading out soon."

Hailey nodded, fully in go mode, but he could see the stress on her face, felt it bone-deep. This could be it. They could be about to save Easton.

Or they might find something none of them wanted to think about.

***

"They tried to cover their IP," Hailey said more to herself than the room as she worked on her computer. Energy buzzed in the office, and she gave Jesse a grateful smile as he placed a steaming container of coffee in front of her. "But we got them."

"That's only half an hour from here." Jesse frowned up at the oversized screen on the wall.

"Oh, shit." Elijah said from his desk. "That address..." He was silent for a moment, then stopped, pulled up a screen next to the one she'd projected. "Whoever you planted that tracker on last night went to that location after banging Alice Silva. Not even half an hour ago."

What the hell? Hailey looked at the matching addresses. Whoever it was had gone to the warehouse, and then there was a login to Easton's account from there?

Shoving up from her seat, she said, "We're going there now. I'm going to pack up the drones. Reese and Elijah, pack up the rest of the gear."

"We need to call the Feds," Jesse said, surprising her.

She paused, looked at him. "Seriously?"

"They have Hostage Rescue Team." AKA HRT. "If Easton is there, they'll have the right gear to infiltrate."

"Fine, but we're going too. I'm not waiting." And they had better gear than the Feds, something she kept to herself because it wasn't the point. And, hell, he was right.

It took barely ten minutes for the five of them to grab all their gear and head out in one of Jesse's spacious SUVs.

While he drove, she sat in the passenger seat, texted Hazel the address of the warehouse, then followed with *Might be Easton's location.*

Her phone rang a moment later. "What the hell?" Hazel demanded.

"I don't know that it's actually where he is, but we were monitoring Easton's Cloud account since Jesse gave us access to it. And someone just logged into it and downloaded all the information. They tried to corrupt the account afterward, but luckily there's a badass firewall...you know what, it doesn't matter. This is where the IP came from."

Hazel was silent for a long moment.

"What?" Hailey demanded.

"You told me that his account was basically unhackable."

"Yeah."

"And now someone logs in and tries to corrupt everything? Are you sure it's not your friend? Maybe he—"

"Maybe he what? Kidnapped himself? You've seen the video."

Hazel cleared her throat. "I know, I'm just saying—"

"I know what you're saying. And Easton didn't do this. We're headed there now—"

"No," Hazel snapped. There were voices in the background, and she said something to someone, but it was too muffled for Hailey to make out. Then she came back on the line. "We've got this handled. I'm headed there with a team, and if we think Easton is in there, then we'll call in HRT."

"Wait, *if* you think?"

"Look, we have to do this by the book."

"How long will it take you to get there?"

"About an hour. Promise you won't do anything."

"Fine." Hailey disconnected, beyond pissed. "Feds are an hour out."

"We'll be there in twenty," Jesse said, not slowing down.

"So what's the plan? Because I'm not waiting on the Feds," Cash said from the back.

"We'll park nearby, scout the place with drones. Then make a decision from there. Even though I hate the idea of letting them take over, the only thing that matters is Easton's safety. I have no ego where he's concerned," Hailey said.

"Yeah, okay, you're right," Cash grumbled.

Jesse, her silent partner, reached out and squeezed her hand once, though he didn't take his eyes off the road. She nearly jolted as she realized she'd thought of him as her partner, but it was true. Even if she was terrified he'd be done with her once she told him everything.

She locked down all those thoughts and focused on the present as they sped down the highway, the cresting sunrise a brilliant show of reds, oranges, and purples as the city around them flickered to life.

CHAPTER 31

—Our friends are our family, and we don't leave family behind.—

"That's eight heat signatures," Hailey murmured, looking at the screen as Jesse flew the drone around the warehouse.

They'd parked at a Waffle House that was open twenty-four hours about a mile away so there'd be no chance of anyone seeing them. Other than a coffee shop and the Waffle House, the rest of the strip mall was closed since it was so early. But the two businesses were doing well thanks to the two hotels flanking the little strip of shops.

The warehouse they were checking out backed up to a drainage/pond area, so no real entrance or exit from there. It had six cameras that they'd spotted and four vehicles in the parking lot. And absolutely no open windows, no way to see inside. The place was new, in an industrial part of town with similar warehouses nearby.

"If Easton is in there, I'd say he's in that far corner," Cash said from the back seat.

Hailey nodded. "I agree." There was a lone heat signature that hadn't been moving much, then another heat signature standing against a wall or door in the same area. The other ones had been moving around freely and in a pattern that indicated they were doing security sweeps.

"It's been more than an hour," Cash added, his impatience mirroring her own.

Yeah, Hailey knew that. She glanced at her phone when it buzzed with an incoming call, saw it was Skye. "Hey, boss."

"We're pulling in next to you. Didn't want to surprise you."

"You're here already?" *Oh, hell, yeah.* Some of the tension that had been weighing her down lifted, and she dragged in a steady breath. She'd never minded being in charge, had fallen into the role of her job naturally. But this job was different because it wasn't a job at all. And she felt the weight of her decisions, knowing that it could mean life or death for Easton, someone she loved. She'd take all the competent backup she could get.

"Yeah, but to be totally transparent, Colt and I headed out earlier this morning. Our job wrapped up, and I wanted to be here for backup in case you needed it. I know how much Easton means to you. So, what's the plan?" she asked as a darkly tinted SUV pulled up next to them.

"I'm still waiting on word from Hazel. She said they'd be here in an hour and that mark passed ten minutes ago."

"Stay on the line. I'm going to call her via three-way."

Despite herself, she snickered.

"Jesus, you're worse than Axel," Skye muttered, but Hailey could hear the laughter in her voice.

"I can't talk right now," Hazel murmured, a buzz of voices in the background as she answered Skye.

"I figured. So where are you, because Hailey said you gave her an hour."

Hailey remained silent, not sure if she should say anything since Skye hadn't specifically said she was on the line.

The silence stretched on the phone, but the voices and hum of energy never wavered. Then things got a lot quieter all of a sudden. "Sorry, had to duck into a supply closet," Hazel said. "Look, I appreciate all Hailey's done, the information she's given us. But we're still waiting on the sign-off from the judge. It's Saturday, and he wasn't at home, but we've hunted him down. As soon as we've got the warrant signed, we're going in. There are a lot of big players involved in this, so we've had to keep the circle of people involved *very* quiet."

"What's the ETA?" Skye asked, her tone neutral.

"I can't answer. Another hour, likely. But our guys are geared up, and we're about to roll out so we'll be close when we get the go-ahead."

"All right, thanks. Talk to you soon."

Hazel ended the call, but Hailey stayed on. "So?"

"Your decision. Wait for them, or we go in. We've got enough sponge grenades to cover us and you guys."

"Hold on." She pressed mute, looked at Jesse and Cash. "Hazel said HRT could be up to another hour. They don't even have the warrant signed yet. There's no reason to think Easton is being harmed right now but—"

"But what if we wait, and it costs him?" Jesse's voice was hard, a mirror for Cash's expression.

Because gone was the easy-going Cash Pierce.

"We could go to jail if this goes sideways."

"We've got the best lawyers," Jesse said. "And I give zero fucks right now."

Cash just nodded his agreement.

Hailey looked at Reese and Elijah, though she already knew the answer. They lived in shades of gray and broke the law all the time. They didn't care either because they made sure people got home to their loved ones and didn't let little things like laws get in their way. "You guys ready?"

Elijah and Reese both nodded, then Reese said, "We're good, and I'm ready to cut the security feeds as soon as you need."

Jesse frowned. "You're not going in."

Hailey cocked her head slightly to the side. "Want to try that again?" Because she had actual experience with infils.

He gritted his teeth, then simply nodded.

She unmuted the phone. "We're good to go. Three of us—Jesse, Cash, and myself—are the ones going in. Reese and Elijah are handling backup and are ready to cut security. And before you ask, Jesse has the training." Something she'd already been over with him on the drive.

Cash had the same military experience as she did—or probably a lot more—but Jesse had trained extensively in Krav Maga, boxing, and had weapons training as well. Not to mention he'd grown up fighting, learning to defend himself. He might be polished now, but the man could throw a punch.

"I know," Skye said.

Okay, then. "Let's do this."

***

"We're ready. On three, two..." Hailey didn't say *one* as she waited for Reese to disable the security.

The five of them were in one SUV, geared up, and ready to go as soon as Reese gave the word from the other vehicle. Hailey and the others had parked in a neighboring lot of a warehouse that was mid-construction. And no one was here today.

"Cameras down for eight minutes," Reese said into their earpieces. "Go!"

Skye had already cut a hole in the surrounding fence so they spilled out of the SUV at once. The five of them wore balaclavas, carried 40 mm grenade launchers which were normally used as riot control weapons. Hailey actually preferred these because they were nonlethal. But the foam rubber bullets they shot packed a hell of a punch. Ask her how she knew.

It was weird to be doing this with Jesse and Cash, but at the same time, not. Because no matter what, these guys were her family in a way no one else would ever be.

Hailey raced ahead to lead and crouched in front of the first door they reached, placed a device on the security panel.

"No heat signature near your entry," Elijah said. "But you've got one incoming. Some of the signatures are moving in different patterns now, likely because of the camera failure."

"10-4." Hailey smiled as the security lock turned green, then grabbed the handle, eased it open.

Skye went in first, Colt right next to her, because they had the most experience out of all of them. Then Hailey and Cash moved in, with Jesse holding up the rear. He'd said he'd wanted to have her six, and holy shit, those words were still rattling around in her head.

They were trying to infil as quietly as possible. Their goal was to get to Easton quickly with no bloodshed. They wanted to incapacitate everyone, but not kill. Because the bastards were going to jail and were going to talk.

Her black rubber boots were silent as she stepped into the clean, white-tiled hallway. The place had an antiseptic scent, like a hospital, but almost immediately she realized this was some sort of lab.

As they hurried down the hallway, she saw open labs and rooms on either side of them, but with no people inside. And no cameras anywhere in sight—which explained why they hadn't been able to hack into anything. They'd tried, but had only been able to find feeds of exterior cameras.

Someone *really* didn't want others to know what was going on in here.

"Heat signature moving in from the left, directly ahead of you." Reese's voice was clipped.

Skye and Colt slowed as they neared the end of the hallway. It T-boned into another hallway with a door directly across from them. Skye held up a fist, and they all stilled as she neared the opening.

Then she stepped out rapidly, launcher in hand, and shot hard and fast.

"Oof!" Someone grunted, but Colt was already in motion, and by the time the three of them had rounded the corner, a man was on the ground, tied up and groaning, duct tape over his mouth.

Jesse grabbed the guy and tossed him into one of the empty rooms, shut the door.

"Cluster of heat signatures to the east of you," Elijah said.

So they all traveled west along the hallway.

Hailey's heart was an erratic tattoo in her chest, but she didn't have to worry about her back, because Jesse had it.

Skye held up her fist again, and they all slowed. Then her boss eased around the next corner, weapon up. She motioned that it was clear.

"There's movement from the corner room," Reese said.

The room they thought Easton was being held in.

"One of the signatures is moving outside, heading your way from the south."

So someone was close, in one of the connected hallways they were about to reach. Which would likely be more doors and glass windows with empty labs—this place was a labyrinth of white walls and floors.

Skye raced forward, the rest of them with her, and when a man in similar gear to them, minus the balaclavas, rounded the corner, Hailey could see the surprise on his face.

But it was too late.

Skye shot at him, slammed the rubber bullet into his chest.

The guy flew back, slamming into the nearby wall with a thud that seemed to reverberate through the hallway.

Colt was on him, securing his arms and mouth, so Hailey and the others moved past him, racing for the corner room.

That just had to have Easton. Because if this had been all for nothing...

Cash moved in front of her, weapon up as he shoved the door open.

Hailey's breath caught in her throat to see Easton sitting at a desk, hunched over a computer.

But he turned to look at the three of them, eyes wide with fear, and, oh shit, of course he was afraid.

She ripped off her balaclava and raced at him. "Come on, let's get you out of here. Feds might be on the way, but we weren't waiting for them. Can you walk?"

He blinked, but nodded, looked to be in a state of shock. Well, yeah, of course he was. Then he seemed to shake himself, and he jumped up off the stool, pulled her into a tight hug.

"Hugs and lots of alcohol later, my man. Let's go." That was Cash.

Nodding, Easton wiped at his eyes but hurried out with them.

"You stay in front of me," Jesse whispered to Easton.

"They're heading in your direction," Reese said over the earpiece, her voice urgent. "Leave the way you came in, and you should avoid them, but go *quickly*. They're moving fast and must know something's up."

Hailey raced along with the others, smiled when she saw Skye pull something from her pocket. C-4 already rigged. Because of course she did.

She motioned for them to run down the hallway as she stayed behind with Colt.

Hailey looked over her shoulder, saw Colt pull out a similar device, secure it to the wall opposite where Skye had placed hers.

There was a shout of alarm behind them from where they'd just come. Yep, they'd been discovered.

Skye and Colt raced after them, and as the sound of gunfire erupted behind them, Skye pressed the button on the detonator.

Heat blasted down the hallway, plaster and glass shattering inward as they ran, but they cleared the hallway, made a sharp left turn.

Almost there.

As they raced toward the exit, a man stepped through one of the doorways, pistol up.

Hailey raised her launcher, but Jesse was faster. He shot the man in his pistol-wielding arm, sending the guy into a spin as he grunted in pain.

She shot him when he made a move for his fallen weapon, right in the chest, the rubber bullet a sharp punch to his solar plexus.

"Feds are close. I just caught the chatter on an off-channel," Reese said. "Hurry!"

As they cleared the warehouse, the six of them sprinted across the parking lot.

"Get out of here," Hailey said to Skye and Colt as they slid through the fence. "You two need to be gone. The three of us will deal with any fallout."

"No—"

"Yes. We don't need any of this tied to Redemption Harbor Consulting at all. Which is why Reese and Elijah are going with you."

Reese was out of the SUV, already shaking her head.

"No!" Hailey snapped. "The three of us have a good reason to be here. And yeah, we might catch some flak. So go, now!" she ordered.

Gritting her teeth, Skye finally nodded. "Let's go," she growled to Colt.

Hailey looked up at Cash and Jesse. "Don't worry, I've got a plan."

CHAPTER 32

—Given the choice again, I'd still make the same decision.—

"Did your plan involve us handcuffed and sitting in the back of a federal agent's SUV?" Cash asked, side-eyeing Hailey.

For some reason, Hailey laughed.

Jesse couldn't figure out why because nothing about this was funny. But she snort-laughed until tears ran down her face.

"Honestly, I lied. I had no plan. I just wanted to get the others out of here," she said, looking out the window of the SUV as a bunch of cuffed guys were being frog-marched to a waiting HRT van. "And we don't know if we're in trouble yet."

Hazel had cuffed the three of them and shoved them in the back of her SUV with orders to "Be quiet!"

Easton was currently sitting in the back of an ambulance, talking to Hazel and an EMT.

"Your nickname should have been *trouble*," Jesse murmured. "That should have been my moniker for you instead of kitten."

"Did you just use the word 'moniker'?" She giggled again, and he wasn't sure why, but the sound was adorable.

"Maybe we could call her Kitten Trouble. Or Trouble Kitten?" Cash suggested.

"Both those sound stupid," Hailey grumbled. "You're stupid."

Cash just laughed as if he didn't have a care in the world.

"My nickname should be badass. Or boss bitch. Or good-ass since I do have a nice ass."

"Not sure who told you that, but they lied," Cash said.

Hailey rammed her shoulder into him in annoyance.

"Why is it that I'm *still* the only adult in the room?" Jesse muttered, gently nudging Hailey. He hated being cuffed, being unable to physically protect her. The adrenaline from earlier had waned, and he simply wanted to hold her—to keep her safe. It was taking everything in him to control the rage at being restrained, helpless. Because they weren't in physical danger, something he was having to remind himself of every few seconds.

Cash let his head fall back. "I'm choosing to believe in justice and—"

"Gah, please shut up." Hailey knocked her knee into his.

"Or what?"

"I'll shut you up myself."

"How are you going to do that?" Cash taunted.

"I swear by all that is holy, you two, I will demand Hazel arrest me if you don't stop," Jesse snarled. They were acting exactly like they had when they'd been in high school.

Thankfully, they both quieted. Mostly.

"He started it," Hailey grumbled, but then she laid her head on Jesse's shoulder.

And he laid his own on hers and closed his eyes, savoring the peace. They might be cuffed and probably going to jail until his lawyer got them out, but Easton was okay, and the four of them were together again.

"Look alive," Cash murmured sometime later.

Jesse opened his eyes, saw the dash showed only twenty minutes had passed. He also saw Hazel stalking toward them. And oooh, she was pissed, given her dark expression.

Her sunglasses covered most of her face, but her jaw was tight as she opened the back door and looked at the three of them. She was silent for a long moment, then said, "Your friend is going to be okay. He's in shock and dehydrated, and they're taking him to Memorial."

"So are we being arrested?" Hailey asked bluntly when Hazel didn't continue.

The other woman shoved her sunglasses up on her head, her eyes icy. "You *should* be."

Huh, that wasn't a *yes*.

"But you have some very powerful friends. Some of whom I'm guessing were here today." She looked between the three of them. "Because someone put in a call to my boss's boss's *boss*."

No one said a word.

"You have anything to say?" Hazel pushed.

"Yeah, snitches get stitches." Hailey's tone was dry as she answered.

"Come on, get out," Hazel finally muttered, motioning to Jesse first. As she unlocked his cuffs, she said, "I want to make it clear that what you all did was beyond reckless. The results could have been very, very different. You're lucky that no one was killed. And," she continued as she unlocked Hailey's cuffs next, "you're lucky that Parker wants the credit for this rescue a hell of a lot more than he wants you dumbasses tossed in jail. Because he's not even complaining about you being let go. He's telling me to take the win."

Now she was working on Cash's cuffs.

"So. Parker gets the credit, along with HRT. None of your names will be going in any reports. And I don't want to see any of you for a good, long while. It's like you were never here. All the assholes who were shot today saw were a bunch of dumbasses in balaclavas. So you're free to go."

"That's it?" Cash asked.

Hailey elbowed him. "Dude, don't push it."

"Yeah, that's it," Hazel snapped. "Now get out of here, and go see your friend."

"What about Senator Silva?" Jesse asked, because he couldn't help himself. "He was behind this. Easton saw him."

In response, Hazel slid her sunglasses onto her face and turned away from them, stalking back to a group of agents wearing blue windbreakers with FBI proudly emblazoned on the backs.

"Come on. Let's go before she changes her mind." Hailey slid her hand into Jesse's, and they headed back to where they'd left their SUV and did exactly what she said—got the hell out of there.

***

"This is ridiculous," Easton grumbled from his hospital bed as he ate the chocolate Jell-o.

"Not ridiculous." Jesse frowned down at his friend even as he was grateful everything had worked out. "They're testing your blood and hair to see if they can figure out what drugs you were given. And you're dehydrated, something you already know. Stop being a baby."

"I'm allowed to be whiny," Easton grumbled again.

Which made Jesse smile. "Yeah, I guess you are."

"See if you can get some more of that Jell-o before we leave." Hailey didn't look up from her phone as she scrolled, looking for any mention of the senator getting arrested. She'd been obsessively checking news and social media sites since they'd arrived at the hospital. "And you're sure you told the Feds about Senator Silva?"

"Pretty sure," Easton said on a tired laugh. "Now what the hell has been going on? You guys busted in there like commandos. Also, who were the other two people with you? Or four, I guess, including the ones in the SUV. I didn't mention them to the Feds, by the way. And why did the Feds let you go? That one agent seemed to know you, Hailey."

"The four people from earlier...I work with all of them," Hailey said as Jesse plucked her phone from her hand and shoved it in his pocket. She frowned, but didn't try to get it back. Instead, she scooted her chair closer to Easton's bed, took his hand in hers, and held it up to her face for a long moment. "We decided we weren't going to wait for HRT to rescue you. And yeah, Hazel was and is quite angry with me. Probably will be for a long time. But I'll live with it because you're alive and here and absolutely nothing else matters."

"That was really dangerous, what you did," Easton rasped out as he squeezed her hand back, his eyes filling with tears.

The door opened, and Cash stepped in, carrying a teddy bear and a big balloon.

"Please tell me you didn't steal that," Hailey said, wiping away a few of her own errant tears.

Cash gave her an affronted look. "I bought this from the gift shop. And the reason I took so long is because I bought balloons for everyone on this floor. They're being delivered right now."

Easton sniffled even more as Cash tied the balloon around the bear's arm and set him on the bed.

"You made him cry!" Hailey grabbed a box of tissues and handed them to Easton.

"No, it's just...being with you all again. At the same time." He covered his face. "Gah, don't look at me! I can't help it. I'm emotional."

Hailey leaned in and hugged him, and Jesse hugged them both. Then he felt Cash wrap his arms around them.

Emotion swelled up inside Jesse, and his own eyes got hot. For this one moment, it was the four of them again.

Then Easton said, "You're not allowed to ghost us again. You know that, right?" His voice was muffled.

"Yeah, I know." Hailey's voice was muffled too. "But I think Cash needs to put on some deodorant." She pulled up from the group hug and made a face.

"I smell great! Why are you being so mean to me?"

"I don't know! All my adrenaline crashed, and now I feel like a ball of anxiety so I'm taking it out on you. I'm sorry. You're just an easy target because you're so stupidly handsome and can obviously take the ribbing. Clearly, you don't stink."

"Did you call me handsome? Are you mocking me now?"

"I was trying to give you a compliment!"

"I forgot what they were like," Easton said to Jesse as Cash and Hailey continued to bicker like actual siblings.

"Me too," Jesse murmured. "I'm glad you're home. And I'd like you to stay at my place for a while. I think there's going to be a media circus once everything comes out, and my house will be more secure." And he wasn't sure if Easton was still in danger.

"Okay."

"Really, no arguments?"

"Nope. The past few days have been...a lot. I'd like to get back to work soon, but Special Agent Blake told me that she was going to have a lot more questions for me and a follow-up. I'm pretty sure once they arrest Senator Silva, that will follow. I think they were just eager to get you guys and me out of there. So..." Easton looked at Hailey, then back at Jesse. Then he mouthed, *You two together?*

Jesse shrugged and then half nodded because he wasn't sure what the hell they were. He knew what he wanted, and she'd said she wouldn't run again. But that didn't mean they were together.

CHapTer 33

—Don't judge me because I'm quiet. No one plans a murder out loud.—

"Ah, the perp walk." Cash grinned as he kicked his feet up on the ottoman in Jesse's living room.

Hailey nodded in approval at the television even as she worked on her laptop. Senator Silva was in cuffs and being walked into the police station while reporters shouted questions at him. The man was keeping his head down, not saying a single word.

Easton was safe, but there were still loose ends they needed to tie up. Silva's fixer, Adam Berch, was still in the wind. So Hailey wasn't stopping until she'd gotten all the answers and was certain Easton was truly safe. When her phone rang, she slid in her Bluetooth. "Hey."

"You guys good?" Skye asked. "I know you weren't arrested but wanted to check in."

"Yeah." Hailey moved her laptop to the coffee table and stood, heading to the kitchen for some privacy. She wasn't sure where the others were, but saw Jesse's phone on the countertop. "Hazel is suuper pissed at us."

"Oh, I know. I already got a call, and so did Leighton." Leighton, another founder of Redemption Harbor Consulting, had served with Hazel and was one of her best friends—had been in her wedding as the "best person." "She'll get over it, but it won't be today. So what are your plans?" Skye asked.

"Ah, I'm going to stay in DC for a little while longer. We've still got some shit to tie up anyway." Like why Easton had all those addresses on his hidden laptop. She still needed to question him about that, but hadn't wanted to overwhelm him at the hospital.

"I figured. Colt and I are going to hang tight for a couple days, so call me if you need anything."

"Thanks." After they disconnected, she let her head roll back, shoved out a sigh. She needed to go find Easton and talk to him. Hell, she needed to find Jesse too. They'd disappeared earlier... Frowning, she glanced at his phone on the countertop when it buzzed with an incoming text.

His screen was locked, but his was like hers and the message popped up anyway before disappearing. But not before she'd read most of the message from a woman named Emily.

It was great to see you in Seattle. Let's set something up soon. We can meet at that little B&B in Virginia? The message was followed by drinks and a winky face emoji.

Huh. Nausea immediately swelled inside Hailey, but she pushed away from the island top. That was so not her business, even if the thought of Jesse with other women made her feel sick. But what the hell did she expect?

Feeling untethered, she headed back to the living room and found Jesse and Easton in there now with Cash.

"How are you doing?" she asked Easton, who'd settled on the love seat, his legs stretched out.

Jesse sat next to her on the larger couch, his leg lining up with hers as he slid an arm around her shoulders.

Easton half smiled. "Good, I swear, so you can stop asking me that."

"No promises... Do you feel up to answering some questions?"

He nodded. "Sure. Fair warning, Special Agent Blake just called and wants to talk to me again."

Yeah, Hailey had figured that was coming soon, especially now that the senator had been arrested. "When you were taken, we found a laptop in your condo."

He gave a ghost of a smile. "I thought that was a good hiding place."

"It was. We just know you. We were able to crack the encryption and ended up finding a bunch of addresses. We visited some of them, and they're all just empty buildings."

Easton blinked in surprise. "Well, you got further than I did in my investigation. I actually thought that was the reason I'd been kidnapped at first. A friend of mine from college, who now works for Innovative Labs, contacted me privately. In person," he added. "They were worried something odd was going on, but didn't think they could trust anyone at work, and rightfully so. She didn't even want to use the phone or leave any sort of electronic trail. Since she knew I'd turned down a job offer from Innovative and trusted me, she reached out. So...what's the deal with the addresses? Are they being used for money laundering? Because that's what my friend was worried about, and I'd only started digging into things."

Hailey nodded. "We think so. The LLCs were set up by an attorney, Ian Warren. Ah, this guy..." She held out her phone, showing him a picture from a recent article. "Do you recognize him?"

Easton shook his head.

Yeah, she hadn't thought so. "We don't know how involved he is, but he set up all the LLCs for Innovative Labs and a bunch of other clients, *including* Henry Silva...which might not matter at all since that's not the reason they took you."

It felt bizarre that Easton had been taken by the senator for his research and knowledge while he'd been sitting on information about potential money laundering, but life was stranger than fiction, something she'd seen play out in her job too many times to count.

"You guys," Reese said, stepping into the living room, a glint in her eyes that Hailey recognized well. She'd been working in the office with Elijah, and clearly she'd found something. "I was still monitoring Alice Silva's line just in case her husband called and...listen to this." She pushed Cash's feet off the ottoman and set the laptop on it before pressing play on the cloning app.

"You better convince him to cut a deal, or he's not going to make it to any trial." Alice Silva's voice was razor-sharp, deadly.

Eyebrows raised, Hailey shot a glance at Jesse, whose expression mirrored her own.

"I can't force him to do anything," the man responded.

"That's Ian Warren," Jesse murmured.

"He's such a moron. Of course you can. You can convince him to do anything, Ian." Her voice was a little more cajoling, sounding more like the woman from the other night who'd invited her lover over to screw her in her husband's bed.

And now Hailey wondered if she was screwing Warren?

Warren sighed, and then things grew silent for a moment.

"Just wait, they're not done," Reese murmured, looking positively gleeful.

"Well...I could promise him a cushy prison sentence. Tell him the judge is going to sentence him harshly, but that I've cut a deal behind closed doors that says he'll have his actual time reduced as soon as the media surrounding everything dies down."

"Oh, that's perfect. And that's what the fool gets for kidnapping that scientist. Seriously, what on earth was he thinking," she growled. "He almost ruined everything with his stupidity! All he had to do was just sit back and let me do the work."

The lawyer sighed. "You know what he's like."

"Unfortunately, I do. And I refuse to go down with his sinking ship because of his stupid ego. I'll visit him and urge him to do what you suggest. Once we convince him to take a deal, I'll find someone to deal with him in prison."

Hailey had a good idea what "deal with him in prison" meant.

Warren paused, then said, "Okay."

"She made a few more calls after that," Reese said, pressing stop. "But nothing to do with her husband or anything. Elijah is still monitoring her calls though."

"So...this is a lot different than what we originally thought. We need to figure out what's going on. And I think I might have an idea how to do it."

"Or we could just let it go," Cash said neutrally. "Easton is free, and it's clear she wasn't involved in his kidnapping. This isn't our circus anymore."

Hailey shook her head. "I don't like loose ends."

"I don't either," Jesse murmured. "What are you thinking?"

So she told them her plan.

CHAPTER 34

—An apple a day keeps anyone away if you throw it hard enough.—

Jesse rolled down the window of his SUV as he parked in front of the closed gates of Senator and Alice Silva's home—though soon he'd be a former senator. A crowd of reporters were gathered across the street, some giving his vehicle curious looks, but it was clear by the two men in suits in front of the gate that they weren't letting anyone too close.

One of the suited men approached Jesse's SUV. "We're not—"

"Tell Alice that Jesse Lennox is here, and I have information she's going to want to talk about." He rolled his window back up, watched as the man spoke into his radio.

Then the gate rolled open as the man waved him through.

The driveway was a half-moon with two entrances. He followed it until he reached the porte cochere and wasn't surprised when another man in a suit approached him.

"Park over there." Not smiling, the man pointed to a small parking area on the side of the house.

Nodding, he did as instructed, and when he got out, the same man was in front of him.

"Hands out, legs apart."

"Seriously?"

"Do I look like I'm joking?"

No, the man did not. Jesse did as he said, his gaze sliding to the house as the man ran a wand over him. He could see Alice watching him from one of the bottom windows. And one of the curtains on the top floor moved slightly, as if someone else was watching.

"Take my phone, and lose your hand." His tone was mild when the guard went to pull his phone out of his pocket.

The man paused, then drew back and motioned for him to follow.

He walked through the foyer, which was all dark, shiny wood, to a sitting room that was a lot lighter than he'd expected. There was more of the same dark wood floors and paneling, but everything else was delicate, feminine furniture in creams and pale blue right down to the silk curtains.

"Normally I would welcome you into my home, but not this afternoon, Jesse." Alice wore a dark blue pantsuit that brought out the blues of her icy eyes. "I understand that one of your employees was..." She seemed to struggle for a moment, then continued. "Kidnapped by my husband. But I'm dealing with a lot right now."

Jesse was glad they were getting right down to it. "I'm going to reach into my pocket and pull my phone out so tell your boy here not to get trigger happy." He hadn't actually seen a gun, but he had no doubt the man was carrying.

"Leave us." She made a shooing motion at the man without even looking at him.

So Jesse pulled out his phone, opened the app Hailey had installed, then pressed play. As the conversation between her and her attorney came over the speaker, her face went ghost pale.

Then Alice cleared her throat, waving her hand for him to stop it. "That's inadmissible in any court. You didn't have my consent."

He snorted softly. "Who said anything about court? I could just drop this on social media and let it play out in the court of public opinion. Warren will almost certainly be disbarred, and your husband...well. I don't think he'll like hearing that you want to send him up the river."

"What do you want?" she gritted out.

"Don't say another word." Adam Berch stepped into the room, holding a weapon. "Toss your phone over here."

Alice jumped up from her seat by the fireplace, clearly startled. "Adam—"

"Quiet, Alice." The familiar way he said her name made Jesse realize that this was the man she'd been having an affair with.

Sighing, she sat back down as Berch stomped on Jesse's phone. Then he said, "Take out the tie pin you've got in."

Gritting his teeth, Jesse did as the man said, tossed it over to him.

The man stomped on it as well, but still didn't lower his weapon. "Why are you really here?"

Sitting back down as casually as he could while having a pistol pointed at him, Jesse looked at Alice. "I wanted to find out if you were involved in the kidnapping of Easton Reed."

She rolled her eyes, her frustration clear. "Adam, put that down. There's no need for that now."

Berch didn't listen, his expression impassive.

Alice let out another sigh, but turned back to Jesse. "Look, you and I don't have to be enemies. I know that scientist works for you, but I had nothing to do with his kidnapping. That was all my dumbass husband."

"But you were behind the bombing at my office." That was more of a guess, but considering it seemed clear that Alice and Berch were working together, it felt like a good one.

She sniffed slightly as she leaned back in her seat. "Of course I wasn't."

"Maybe, maybe not." He looked at Berch now.

The other man's eyes narrowed, but he didn't respond.

Okay, so Jesse was going to have to push harder. "The Feds are looking for you."

"I've heard." His tone was neutral.

"They've got video of you talking to David Beeker, giving him a payoff to bomb my company. And he's willing to testify against you."

"There's no video."

"Oh, because you think that asshole bartender actually deleted it? Nope." Jesse gave him an obnoxious smile, one he used occasionally in the boardroom to show that he had all the cards.

Now the wheels were turning in Berch's head.

"Wait, what?" Alice looked between the two of them now, true shock in her icy eyes. "Tell me you weren't involved with any of my husband's schemes. Please tell me, Adam." There was a pained note in her voice, one that spoke of betrayal.

Oh yeah, they were sleeping together all right.

Berch looked at her, and Jesse could see that, oops, he *had* been working with the senator. At least on this. "We'll talk about it later."

"No, we'll talk about it right now." She snatched a glass half full of water off the side table and threw the entire glass into the crackling fireplace, smashing it against the brick interior. A sharp sizzle and pop followed. "I'm so sick of dealing with incompetent men!"

She turned to Jesse, her eyes wide and a little wild as her civilized veneer slid away. "I had nothing to do with your employee's kidnapping or the bombing at your office. The only thing I'm guilty of is doubling my husband's campaign contributions."

Ah, so she'd been working with Warren on the loan-back schemes.

"We were funneling some of his money into bogus R&D—"

"Shut up, Alice!" Berch tried to physically shove her back in her seat, but she tossed his hand off.

"No, I will not shut up. I'm so sick of you telling me what to do. And it's not like you're going to let him walk away after this so I'm going to tell someone how smart I am."

Holy shit. Jesse kept his mouth shut as she turned back to him.

And she did sit, looking a lot more like the Alice he'd known over the past few years as she faced him. "All my poor, stupid husband had to do was nothing.

That's it. Simply sit back and let me take care of everything. I looked the other way while he screwed his whores because he's got a face that voters like, and he's easy to manipulate. I won't explain what we were doing with the money because I'm sure you already know."

Jesse nodded. "A loan-back scheme. Then you were taking the funds and investing them into Innovative Labs?"

"Exactly. They're close to finding a cure for ALS, and once they do, it will—or would have been—leaked that Henry was personally funding a lot of the research. The headlines would have written themselves. Instead he got it into his dumb head..." She shot Berch a withering glare before she turned back to Jesse. "That he could force some scientist to, I don't know, research faster. Jesus, what a fool," she muttered. "All he had to do was be patient. That's it. Be patient and do nothing," she repeated her earlier sentiment. "But he let his ego get carried away with him, just like always. And it's not the first time either. He ran our finances into the ground before, but I saved us. Me! I even let him think it was all his idea to work with Innovative Labs, but..." She sighed, looking exhausted as she stood. "I can't deal with this anymore. Just take him away," she growled to Berch before stalking from the room.

"Get up," Berch ordered, his gun firmly trained on Jesse. Then he pulled out a pair of flex-cuffs, tossed them over. "And put these on."

"Nah, I'm not gonna do that." He slid them into his front pocket instead.

Berch blinked once, before his eyes narrowed. "Fine, I'll just shoot you right here."

"Sure, you're gonna shoot me with a bunch of reporters across the street, in Alice's nice living room filled with valuable antiques."

"Her house is well insulated. And even though she doesn't want to deal with the cleanup of your blood, she'll just have to." Berch gave a dark smile.

"I don't think you'll be able to clean up all my DNA. And since a bunch of people, literal reporters who likely took pictures, saw me enter, this would be considered my last known whereabouts. Not to mention my assistant knows I'm here." Not true, but whatever. "As well as a handful of my employees. Is killing me really the right choice?"

Sirens sounded nearby, and he breathed out a sigh of relief. The Feds had wanted him to wear an earpiece, but he'd declined since he figured it would have been found. They'd planted two cameras on him and a listening device, hoping that Berch would see one and think it was all Jesse had on him.

The plan had worked.

"You son of a bitch," Berch snarled.

"Sure am. And your best bet is to run while you still can. Chances are you'll be able to avoid the Feds if you leave now. Because I guarantee you've got a vehicle parked nearby."

Berch wavered for a moment, but then he straightened, and Jesse saw the murderous intent in his eyes. Apparently he'd miscalculated this one. "No reason I need to leave you alive."

"Think again, asshole!"

Berch, startled, half turned, but it was too late. Holding a canister of bear spray, Hailey nailed him in the face at full blast.

His scream filled the air as she unleashed her wrath on him. Jesse charged, slamming Berch into the brick by the fireplace even as he grasped the man's arm in a death grip, smashed it against the brick.

Berch snarled, attempted to fight back, but dropped his gun as he screamed in pain from the capsaicin. Moving like he'd been trained, Jesse tossed the guy on the ground, yanked his arms behind his back and flex-cuffed him.

"Holy shit." Breathing hard, likely from adrenaline, Hailey stared down at them, ignoring Berch's groans as much as he was. "That was an awesome take-down. You moved like a pro."

At that moment, the front door busted open, and Hazel, along with a handful of other FBI agents, streamed in, weapons up, shouting orders.

Hailey dropped the bear spray and held her hands up, but Jesse simply shoved himself up from the floor and grasped her arm.

"What the hell are you doing here, Hailey?" Hazel demanded as one of her agents grabbed Berch from the floor and started reading him his rights.

The man just moaned in agony in response.

"I hid in the back of the SUV," Hailey said right as Cash walked in with a restrained Alice Silva, her hands behind her back.

Her mouth was pulled into a thin line, and the only thing she said was, "I want my lawyer."

"Caught her trying to sneak out the back," Cash said, grinning as he nudged the woman forward.

Hazel blinked at him. "Is that a sandwich?"

He shrugged, holding up a half-eaten...yep, ham and cheese sandwich. "I was hungry."

Hazel looked between the three of them, blinking in a way that made him think she was going to drink an entire bottle of wine after work.

"They weren't going to stay back while I came in wired. So I didn't try to stop them," Jesse explained. He'd just opted not to tell the Feds that they'd been hiding in his vehicle after he'd confirmed the plan with Hazel and Special Agent Parker.

"Yeah, we don't listen to orders very well." This from Hailey, who then fist-bumped Cash.

Fist-bumped him.

"You could have told me, and we'd have..." Hazel threw her hands up. "You know what, I don't care. You reached out to me, so I'm calling this a win. You all helped bring down what is turning out to be a criminal conspiracy of money laundering, murder, kidnapping, what sounds like fraud, and probably more things I'm not thinking of. So. Get your asses back in your SUV and meet me down at the office. Because you're all making statements, *not* talking to the reporters out there, and we're getting this paperwork out of the way tonight. Unless any of you need medical care?"

They all shook their heads as a forensics expert bagged the dropped bear spray as part of evidence.

"Did you actually make the sandwich? Or was it already prepped?" Hailey asked Cash as she leaned in to hug Jesse tight and bury her face against his chest.

He held her back, closed his eyes even as Cash answered. "There's a whole platter of them in the kitchen. They look like leftovers from some fancy brunch or something. We should grab some on the way out."

"There's something wrong with you two," Jesse murmured.

"Are you just realizing that?" Cash asked, slinging an arm around Jesse for a quick side hug. "I'm glad you're okay. Took everything I had to hold Hailey back from going Cujo on Berch too early."

Her eyes flinty, Hailey nodded as she looked up at him. "I really, really wanted to shoot him, but common sense won out."

"Now that bastard is going to go to jail for a hell of a long time." Hopefully forever.

CHaPTer 35

—When someone does something wrong, don't forget all the things they did right.—

Two days later

Curled up on Jesse's couch, her head on his shoulder, Hailey looked up as Hazel entered the living room to address the four of them. Jesse's security had let her in, and they were all glad to see her.

Reese and Elijah had returned to North Carolina and were now helping the rest of their team prep some new job that Hailey was sitting out for. Because she planned to spend some time with Jesse that didn't involve trauma and worry for their friend's life. She wanted to just *be* with him. Something she really needed to tell him.

Cash was sitting next to Easton—where he'd been practically glued to the man's side for the past almost forty-eight hours. Well, they all had been, and she was pretty sure they were making Easton crazy with their hovering.

"Do you want anything to drink?" Cash asked, standing. "Jesse's got everything you can imagine."

She gave them a tired half smile. "I'm good, but thanks. I just wanted to stop by and fill you in on everything personally since you were so helpful-ish with this case." Her gaze lingered on Hailey for a long moment.

"Before you tell us everything, are we good?" Hailey motioned between the two of them, because she truly did care. She adored Hazel and didn't want bad blood between them.

"Yeah, you lunatic," Hazel said on a laugh. "I should start calling you Skye 2.0."

"That's literally the nicest thing anyone has ever said to me." Jumping to her feet, Hailey pulled the agent into a tight hug, but as she stepped back, she added, "And also not true. She's in a class by herself. One I only aspire to."

Before Hailey had met her, before the creation of Redemption Harbor Consulting or Security, Skye had busted her friend out of a Mexican cartel's clutches single-handedly. Skye was like life goals, but she would take the Skye 2.0 compliment.

"Yeah, probably a good thing we don't have two Skyes running around."

Or more like a bad thing, because the world would be a better place. But Hailey simply sat back down with Jesse, leaning into his embrace as he automatically wrapped his arm around her to pull her close. Yeah, she was right where she wanted to be.

"So..." Sighing, Hazel collapsed onto a cushy, tufted dark blue chair. "This is all off the record, by the way. We're still sifting through a lot, but Alice Silva is the one who originally hired Berch years ago. Everyone has always assumed he's Henry's fixer. Which he essentially is, but he does Alice's bidding and cleans up after Henry. Until recently."

She shook her head, but continued.

"It's a giant clusterfuck, but from what we've gathered, Alice set up various LLCs years ago working in conjunction with one of the CEOs at Innovative Labs—oh, he's going down too, by the way. Already lawyered up, but it won't matter. Her attorney, Ian Warren, did all the legwork, and while he's smart, he's not perfect. We've been doing a forensic accounting of all his files associated with the Silvas and anyone remotely connected to this growing case."

"Did she really not know about the senator kidnapping me?" Easton murmured.

"I don't think she did," Alice said. "She's far too angry at him over it and blames him for ruining everything. And she's not wrong. It's highly unlikely we'd have caught wind of the scam she was running. She was taking more than half of his campaign donations, running them through a shell corporation via her LLCs, doubling the donations, then replacing the original ones right where they were supposed to go. The profit of her illegal scheming was going to fund cutting-edge research. Well, some of it. Because one of her partners was using his cut to funnel it through the fake R&D companies. AKA the empty buildings you found."

She shook her head in disgust.

"Honestly, it's so convoluted I'm not a hundred percent sure I'm even explaining this properly, but thankfully I work with a lot of really smart people who are ripping the Silvas' finances apart. At the end of the day, Senator Silva thought kidnapping you would kick-start the research they were already funding. But he didn't tell his wife. And Alice is so pissed at her lover for working with Henry, that she's rolling over on everyone. She'll end up doing time, but because she's been so forthcoming with everything and she wasn't involved in the bombing or kidnapping..." Hazel shook her head. "She's going to cut a deal, but the others are going down hard."

"Will any of us need to testify?" Jesse asked.

"At this point, I don't think it's going to trial. No one involved in this wants more publicity, but we'll see. We got Berch on camera and audio attempting to kill you. And Henry Silva and Berch are both going down for the bombing because Berch rolled on Henry with very little pressure. Your name," she said, looking at Jesse, "might come out in some of this because he tried to kill you at the Silvas' home, but you're just a tiny blip in what's turning out to be a huge scandal." She stood, clearly wrapping up. "Hailey and Cash, you shouldn't be mentioned at all. Easton...I'm sincerely glad that you're okay."

She shook his hand once before heading out, but not before telling Hailey she'd call her next time she was in North Carolina.

"Well, that was a whole lot," Hailey murmured, not sure she understood everything either. But she didn't really care because all her people were safe. That was the only thing that mattered.

"I'm selling my construction company," Cash blurted into the silence.

Blinking, Hailey looked at him, as did Jesse and Easton.

"Since when?" Jesse asked, pulling Hailey even closer.

Which, at this point she was about to crawl into his lap. Something she really wanted to do. But not in front of an audience.

"I've already got a couple offers. I haven't looked at any of them because of everything that's been going on, but I'd put word out a couple weeks ago."

"Wow, that's exciting. Congratulations." Hailey grinned at him. "So now you're going to be even richer."

He just lifted a shoulder, but didn't smile.

She frowned, worried she'd offended him for real. "I'm just playing, Cash."

"I know. I...I reached out to Skye to talk to her about a job."

Hailey blinked in surprise, looked up at Jesse, who looked just as taken off guard as she. "Wow. That's... Well, what did she say?"

"I just finished a Zoom interview with her and a couple of her partners about an hour ago. She wants me to come on board and said I could choose my location... I'd like to work in North Carolina with you, but only if it's not going to be an issue."

"Are you serious?" she asked even as she jumped up to tackle-hug him.

Laughing lightly, he hugged her back. "I wasn't sure what your reaction would be."

"Obviously you interviewed with her so she must have already done a really deep dive on you. You...*know* what we do, right?" He clearly had to, or Skye never would have agreed to bring him on board. Because their work wasn't conventional, even if they'd created their companies to look that way.

"You help people who can't afford it, who have no one to turn to, take down assholes who think they're above the law—while simultaneously breaking the law. And I'll get to put all my former skills to good use."

"It's going to be a big change from what you've been doing."

He lifted a shoulder. "Look, I love working on things with my hands, creating things. And I love giving people good homes, a place to sleep at night. But I've been feeling this way for a while. I just didn't know what the hell to do with myself so I kept working."

"This is a whole lot to digest." And it just added another layer of tension to her already busy thoughts. Mainly because she wasn't sure what the hell was going to happen with her and Jesse. She was excited Cash was coming on board, but...what did any of this mean for Jesse? Because while she loved her job, she knew she'd give it up for him, move here for him if he asked.

"Well, while you digest my news, Easton and I are going to lunch." Cash stood, slapping Easton gently on the shoulder.

"We are? Oh, yep, we are." Easton stood, nodded at the two of them. "But Hailey, you and I are having a movie marathon tonight."

"Definitely," Hailey murmured, turning to straddle Jesse as the other two left. "And now we're all alone," she murmured.

His hands flexed on her hips as he watched her closely. As if he was trying to see right through to her innermost thoughts.

She rolled her hips over his growing erection, desperate for more of him—even if they'd already had sex twice earlier that morning. She felt consumed with the need to make up for lost time. Maybe because she was afraid their time together was coming to an end.

He groaned softly as he reached for the hem of her sweater, pulled it over her head. And his groan grew when he saw the half corset she'd worn. She'd borrowed it from Reese because she didn't have anything like this—though she planned to change that very soon.

To her surprise, he didn't make a move to touch her further, or strip off the rest of her clothes. And when she went to take off his T-shirt, he stilled her hands.

"What?" she asked, confused.

"We're all safe now, and I want answers, Hailey. I know I said that I didn't need to know all your secrets, but is there more to the reason you left me? Because it felt like you were holding back before. I didn't push because it seemed like the wrong time. But I am asking now."

On instinct, she tried to move off him, but he gripped her hips hard, held her tight so that she remained straddling him.

"No. Running." His words were a soft growl.

Gently she set her hands on his shoulders, but didn't make eye contact. She couldn't. Instead she looked at a spot on the couch behind him.

But he wasn't having it. Gripping her chin, something she wouldn't allow another human being on earth to do, he forced her to look at him. "Talk. I'm not going anywhere."

Yeah, he said that now. "I...about a week before I ended things, I found out I was pregnant," she blurted, the words coming out in a rush.

He stared, his mouth falling open a fraction.

So she forced herself to get the rest of the words out as fast as possible. "I was terrified even though I'd been thinking I might be. I was really late for my period, so I finally worked up the courage to get a test. Actually, I got five of them, and they all came back positive. You were gone on a college tour when I found out, so I threw away all the evidence. I was horrified, knowing that a pregnancy was going to ruin everything. I..." Swallowing hard, she forced herself to talk past the tightness in her throat. "Before I could tell you, I lost it. It all happened so quickly and..."

She swallowed back more tears, wishing he'd say something.

"Mother Nature made the decision for us, but in that moment I knew I could never risk getting pregnant again. It would have destroyed your future." She'd wanted a baby with him, but had known deep down how selfish that was. Because she'd wanted a piece of him forever, someone to love unconditionally.

He cursed softly and swiped his thumbs across her cheek, making her realize she was crying. "A baby wouldn't have ruined anything," he murmured, kissing her gently, his lips barely skating over hers. "It would have made things more complicated, but not ruined anything. And I hate that you dealt with all that alone."

More tears fell now in a free fall, but she forced herself to continue. "You don't understand how selfish I am! I was sad I lost the baby. Depressed. Because I wanted that with you, something to hold on to when you moved on to bigger and better things. What kind of asshole thinks like that? It's why I did what I did." She'd run because she'd known that if she stayed, she'd have turned into a selfish asshole just like her mother always said she was.

"I never would have moved on to something bigger or better because there is nothing better than you," he snarled. "You've always been mine, Hailey. *Always*. And there's never been anyone else for me. And you weren't an asshole. You were a young adult who'd spent most of your years in foster care after your piece-of-shit mother overdosed. Cut that traumatized teen that you were a break because the Hailey I knew then, and now, is *amazing*. Selfless. And you're not walking away again. I won't let you," he growled before he captured her mouth with his.

Too stunned to do anything else with his response, she leaned into him as he teased his tongue against hers and stripped her like a man possessed.

Her entire body pulsed with awareness, heat pooling at her core as he removed her clothes with a single-minded determination.

They were both naked in moments, but he had her right back where she'd been before, straddling him and gripping her hips as if he dared her to try to move.

He claimed her mouth again as he cupped the back of her head in a dominating grip. As he teased her mouth, she went up on her knees, centering herself over his thick erection.

He thrust up even as she started to rock onto him. They moved in a frantic rhythm, him holding on to her so tight she knew she'd have bruises on her hips. But she didn't care.

After he'd freed her from years of guilt, pent-up shame, she knew she'd give up everything for him. Because some things would never change. He'd seen her at her worst and still accepted her for who she was. He accepted all of her.

And as their bodies continued moving in that timeless cadence, she gripped onto his shoulders, digging her fingers in hard. She wanted to mark him as much as he'd marked her. Of course he'd marked her in places no one would ever see, this man who'd stolen her heart nearly a decade ago.

As he continued to thrust, his thick length filling her, stretching her, she felt as if she would burst into a million pieces. But when he reached between their bodies, teased her pulsing clit, she let go of everything: the past, her fears, guilt. Truly let go.

She climaxed harder than she ever had as she rode the man she loved. There would be no running ever again. Before she'd come down from her high, he joined her, burying his face against her neck as he lost himself inside her.

She felt the scrape of his teeth against her skin as he thrust harder, harder into her, and had never felt so whole in her entire life. Being with him was like coming home.

He *was* her home. Always had been.

It had just taken her a while to figure it out.

CHAPTER 36

—There is no plan B. He's the only choice.—

"Hey sleepyhead," Easton said as Hailey strode into the kitchen, feeling better than she had in years.

She'd slept like the dead last night, and it was all thanks to Jesse. After they'd christened his couch yesterday afternoon, the others had returned not too long after. They'd gotten takeout, reminisced, and swum in Jesse's giant-ass *heated* pool. She and Easton had watched a movie, and then she and Jesse had excused themselves for some privacy.

And he'd basically banged her into a coma-like sleep.

"It's only eight," she grumbled around a yawn.

Before she could move toward the coffeepot, Easton waved her off. "I've got you covered. I'm tired of everyone taking care of me, so let me get yours."

"Okay, I won't argue." Yawning again, she sat at the island top and looked around. "Where is everyone?"

"Cash is off to a meeting. About selling his business, I think—he was in very fancy duds. And Jesse didn't want to wake you. He told me to tell you that he's gone into the office for a few hours, but he'll have his phone on him."

"I need to invest in whatever those two do, and I'll be set for life," she murmured.

Easton laughed lightly as he set her coffee in front of her. "Very true. I'm probably headed back to my condo tomorrow. I need to start getting back into a routine, and Jesse said my place is as good as new. No trace of any bear spray or wall damage."

"Oh, hell, I'd forgotten about that." She lightly laughed as she took a sip of her coffee. "You remember how I take it."

"Of course... So. You and Jesse? What's going on with you two? Did you finally move past whatever issues held you back years ago?"

Swallowing hard, she shifted slightly in her chair but didn't put her coffee down. She chose her words as she took another sip, savored the rich aroma. "I did and he...well, he accepts all of me."

"He always did."

"Yeah, I realize that now." But she'd been a traumatized teen dealing with years of emotional and occasionally physical abuse from a drug-addicted mother. A woman who'd never deserved that moniker. "I wish I'd been smart enough to realize it all those years ago. And for the record, I'm sorry for ghosting you too." She forced herself to meet her friend's gaze. "You were one of my best friends and deserved better."

"I knew it wasn't about me, or any of us," Easton said quietly in that kind way of his. "And if there was any forgiveness needed, I did it a long time ago."

She blinked away a rush of heat to her eyes, cursing all these tears she seemed to be shedding lately. It was like the floodgates had opened and she couldn't stop them. "So when do you think you'll go back to work?"

"As soon as possible. Jesse has another workspace for my team set up already, and I'm ready to dive back into my research. I think it'll help with processing everything. I keep waking up thinking I'm..." He shook his head. "It could have been worse. That's what I keep telling myself."

Sliding off the stool, she moved over and pulled him into a big hug. "Maybe talk to someone about it? Don't let it build up." Something she wished she'd known to do a long time ago.

"Oh, don't worry, I've already set up an appointment with my therapist."

"Why am I not surprised?" she asked on a laugh. He'd always been the problem solver and pragmatist of all of them. As she sat back down at the island, her phone buzzed with an incoming call. "I'm gonna grab this, okay?" she murmured even as she answered. "Skye, hey. Everything okay?"

"Yeah, just checking in with you—and no rush on coming back to work. Your team is a well-oiled machine. But I know we haven't had a chance to talk about Cash joining the company or anything else. We're headed back today, so I wanted to see if you wanted to catch a ride, grab some of your things, and then get back to your man while you figure out the future."

"That sounds...amazing, actually. Yeah, okay thanks. When are you leaving?"

"Wheels up whenever we feel like it, but we're ready."

"Give me, like, half an hour? I just need to change, and I'll catch a ride to meet you."

"See you soon." It was still really early, so if she caught a ride on Brooks's jet—another of the founders—it wouldn't take her long to pack up then head back here. Because she wanted to grab some of her things and to check in with her team, especially since she was thinking of taking a serious chunk of time off.

She called Jesse to tell him, but it went straight to voicemail.

"He's in meetings," Easton said, clearly having seen who she called.

"Do you mind passing on a message to him? I'm going to catch a ride home with my boss, pick up my stuff, then head back to DC. I'll probably be back before he returns, but in case he beats me or I can't get a hold of him, will you let him know?"

"Of course. I'm glad you two figured things out finally."

She started to say that they hadn't totally figured things out yet, but smiled instead. "Me too." Because they were going to figure things out, no matter what.

CHaPTer 37

—I will always choose her.—

Jesse froze mid-knock as Hailey's front door flew open.

She blinked, clearly surprised to see him. "Hey...what—"

He moved fast, crushing his mouth to hers as he guided her backward into her house, pushing her up against the nearest wall. He felt possessed with the need to touch her, hold her in his arms.

She arched into him, wrapping her legs around him as he ate at her mouth. And while he wanted to take her right on the floor, he tore his lips away, stared down at her.

"You *ran*," he growled as pain and betrayal punched through him. After yesterday he'd thought things were different, that they were on the same page.

Blinking dazedly, she shook her head. "No, I was coming back to get my stuff."

And that was when he saw the two suitcases in the foyer. Two very big ones.

"I told Easton, and I tried calling you a bunch of times, but it kept going to voicemail. I even texted."

"I had to get a new phone after Berch destroyed mine, and the new one is—it doesn't matter. Easton said you'd left." And his heart rate had only just returned to normal now that she was in his arms again.

"Wait...*what*?" She stared at him in shock. "He said I'd left? As in I left you?"

"He said you'd gone home." And now that he thought about it... "He said that I should follow you and figure things out."

"He *knew* I was coming back though," she insisted, frowning now. "What the hell is wrong with him? I want to be mad at him, but...he was so sweet when we talked this morning." She shook her head, mostly sputtering, and he eased back to let her down.

Jesse whipped out his phone, put it on speaker and called Easton—who picked up on the first ring.

"What the hell is wrong with you!" shouted Hailey before Jesse could get a word out.

"I basically told Jesse you ran so he'd chase after you."

"Wh... *why*?" Jesse demanded.

"Because you didn't get to a decade ago, and I thought it would be cathartic. And you two need to sit down and talk about the future without any distractions—and I figured it'd force *you* to do something you want to do but are trying to convince yourself to wait on. Because I'm not watching you two waste any more time in your lives. You're welcome." He hung up.

Still blinking in surprise, Hailey looked up at Jesse. "Did you drive here?"

"Flew." And he could finally breathe again. Because Hailey hadn't left him. No, she'd been coming back to him.

"Want to come in for a bit? See my place while we talk shit about Easton?"

He let out a startled laugh and nodded, following her deeper into the one-story cottage tucked away in a historical part of the small downtown. "This place looks like you."

"Yeah?" When she looked at him, he saw the hesitation in her tawny brown eyes.

Everything was tidy, but not obsessively neat. And there was so much color everywhere. Bright throws, funky art on the walls, and a whole lot of books everywhere.

He nodded while absently patting his jacket pocket to reassure himself that the jewelry box was still there.

"Listen, he's right," Hailey hedged as she led him into her kitchen, which was mostly grays and whites.

But the extras were all bright colors, which made sense. Hailey had always loved color and it was clear she'd stamped herself all over this house. And he wanted her to put her stamp on him.

"We do need to talk," she continued.

His gut tightened as he watched her play with her long hair, a nervous habit.

"I'm just going to say it. I love you," she blurted. "I never stopped loving you and I'm never going to stop. I was going to die old and alone, Jesse Lennox. Because I could never move on from you. Not when you took my heart. I kept trying to tell you over the past couple days, but it was always during sex, and I thought you might not believe me. So I was going to come back with my suitcases, tell you that I'm moving in and that I love you. You're not getting rid of me...*ever*." She crossed her arms over her chest, as if she expected an argument.

Reaching out, he took her hands in his, then slid the custom-made sapphire ring he'd been out buying today onto her ring finger. Because he hadn't gone into the office, he'd gone to his jeweler.

"I love you too, Hailey West. I never stopped either. And I didn't try to move on because what would be the point? You're going to marry me, and we'll decide where to live. It doesn't have to be in Virginia. I only settled there for business, but I can live anywhere, and I want you to be happy. So we'll move here, and you'll keep working for Redemption Harbor if that's what you want. But if you don't want to work, you don't have to either. I want you to have everything you've ever wanted, including a dog. You and I will be adopting one from a shelter as soon as possible. And I'm taking you to Paris on our honeymoon because I know you've always wanted to go there. I want to create a real life with you, to live with you, wake up to your gorgeous face every morning, and grow old with you."

She threw her arms around him, kissing him hard as she basically shoved him against her refrigerator. "You didn't actually ask me to marry you," she finally murmured as she pulled back to look up at him, a grin teasing her lips.

He kept his arms tight around her, needing the contact with her. They'd spent far too many years apart. Lonely years where all he'd done was want to be with her. "I'm still not asking. You're marrying me."

"And you're very bossy."

"You like it."

Her cheeks flamed, but she grinned. "So Easton *was* pretty smart, huh?"

"I'd planned to wait for the right time to propose—"

"Not a proposal."

"—and he pushed up my timeline, so yeah, he's a genius."

She grinned, then paused. "I have one more sort of confession to make. I saw a text message on your phone—I wasn't looking! A text popped up when everything was going on with Easton, and it was some woman asking to meet you at a B&B or something, and I fully admit that I'm jealous even thinking about it, but—"

"That's not an ex, just a woman I had a few meetings with last time I was in Seattle. She's pushy as hell and keeps asking to meet up at various places, but you have nothing to worry about. And you can have full access to my phone. The code is my face or your birthday."

Those big eyes blinked once. Twice. "Seriously?"

"Yep."

"I don't need access to your phone. I trust you."

"Well, you've got it anyway. I want to start fresh with you with no secrets. And I want to get married as soon as possible."

"Okay."

Now he was the one to blink. "Okay?"

"I'm not going to argue with you. I love you, Jesse. I'd do a courthouse wedding right now if you wanted."

For a brief moment he was tempted, but no. She deserved a giant party, a gorgeous dress, and to be surrounded by her friends. Once upon a time, he'd promised to give her everything and he was going to live up to that promise.

"Two months. We'll get married in two months. That way we can plan a long honeymoon where we're naked the entire time."

She threw her head back and laughed, the joyous sound wrapping around him and infusing him with the purity of it. "Two works for me, but I bet we could plan it in one."

EPILOGUE

Two weeks later

"I'm going to apologize in advance for these assholes," Elijah said, no heat in his voice as he and Jesse approached the door to the pub. "Fair warning, they're going to haze you or some stupid shit. But they really *are* good guys."

Jesse wasn't worried because these were Hailey's people. And she'd wanted him to meet them before the wedding, so here he was, about to meet some of the men she worked with—and had served with. They were like her brothers, so this mattered.

"It's fine. I get it." These guys thought of her as one of their own, and he was this new guy coming in out of nowhere. Though not technically new since he'd known her longer than they had, but he definitely understood that urge to protect her. He'd have to pay his dues, let them see that he was in this for the long haul with her.

As they stepped into the bar, he saw that it was just four guys at a high-top near the pool tables and dart boards. And a bartender who simply nodded at them. Frowning, Jesse glanced around.

The place was a basic bar with all quality wood, seating, custom lighting, a full bar... The place should be packed at six. Instead it was empty.

As he approached the high-top table, a huge man with a thick beard who was the same height as Jesse but as broad as a barn door stood, stared him down for a long moment. Then his weathered face broke into a huge grin, and he held out a meaty hand. "Jesse Lennox, it's a pleasure to meet you. Always wanted the chance to meet the one who mailed Hailey all those care packages and letters."

"Yeah," another one from the table nodded. "She always shared too. Said you and her foster brothers were the best. We own this place and closed it down for the night so we could all get to know each other."

"Every round is on us," a third added, holding up his half-empty beer. "We're looking forward to the wedding too. Already got my tux."

The fourth lifted his beer too, nodded. "To the man who created multiple apps just for the military and transitioning military. You made life a hell of a lot easier for all of us. We're glad you finally locked Hailey down because she deserves to be happy more than anyone I know, and she's been nothing but sunshine the past couple weeks."

Jesse stared in surprise at the warm welcome, wondering if they were messing with him, given Elijah's dire warning.

"What the hell!" Elijah looked at the four of them indignantly, shouting before Jesse could even think about responding. "You assholes shaved off my eyebrows our first night out!"

The big one just laughed and threw his head back. "Shit, you'll never let us forget that. I've said I'm sorry a hundred times. It just means we like you."

"Screw you, Rowan! You're buying all my drinks too. And appetizers."

The big man clapped Elijah on the shoulder with a laugh. "Fine, fair enough if you stop bringing up the whole eyebrow thing."

Jesse sat at the high-top table as the men introduced themselves one by one. Rowan was the big one headed to the bar with a grumbling Elijah, and the others were Ezra, Bradford and Tiago. At first he thought they might have been screwing with him, but nope, they were welcoming him with open arms.

A couple hours later the bar door opened again with a bang and Hailey, Reese, and a few others he vaguely recognized as her co-workers strode in. Including Cash, who was watching Reese with more than coworker vibes.

Hailey made a beeline for Jesse and practically jumped into his lap. "Have they been okay? Elijah was worried they'd shave your head or something."

He laughed, brushing his lips over hers. "Either they're incredible actors and are lulling me into a false sense of security, or they're truly welcoming me to your family."

"You're my family," she murmured. "Always have been."

Rowan strode up then, slung an arm around Jesse's shoulders, beer wafting off him as he grinned. "He's all right, Hailey. We're keeping this one."

"Good thing, or I'd have to kick your ass," she said, snagging his beer from him.

Which just made Rowan roar with laughter. "Always threatening violence, short stuff."

"Asshole!" Elijah shouted from the dart boards, making the big man laugh even harder. The man looked terrifying, but Hailey had been right, he was like a teddy bear. One who could probably kill someone twelve different ways and make it look like an accident.

"Okay, they really *do* like you," she murmured as Rowan made his way to one of the pool tables, greeting Cash in a way that said those two had definitely gotten off on the right foot.

"I am very likeable."

"And lickable," she murmured, her eyes going hot.

He blinked at her words. "You want to lick me? Let's get out of here right now, then."

Laughing, she threw her arms around his neck. "I didn't actually mean right now, but okay, let's go. We can fool around in that huge SUV of yours and come back, or just go home."

He'd had fun tonight, and was glad to get to know her friends, but he liked the sound of home.

Home, with Hailey, where he'd always belonged. And soon he was going to have a new tattoo on his arm—with the date he would marry the woman he'd always loved.

Dear Readers

Thank you for reading my latest book! If you'd like to stay in touch and be the first to learn about new releases you can:

Check out my website for book news and social media information: https://www.katiereus.com

Also, please consider leaving a review at one of your favorite online retailers. It's a great way to help other readers discover new books and I appreciate all reviews.

Happy reading,
Katie

ABOUT THE AUTHOR

Katie Reus is the *USA Today* bestselling author of the Red Stone Security series, the Ancients Rising series and the Redemption Harbor series. She fell in love with romance at a young age thanks to books she pilfered from her mom's stash. Years later she loves reading romance almost as much as she loves writing it.

However, she didn't always know she wanted to be a writer. After changing majors many times, she finally graduated summa cum laude with a degree in psychology. Not long after that she discovered a new love. Writing. She now spends her days writing paranormal romance and romantic suspense.

COMPLETE BOOKLIST

Ancients Rising

Ancient Protector

Ancient Enemy

Ancient Enforcer

Ancient Vendetta

Ancient Retribution

Ancient Vengeance

Ancient Sentinel

Ancient Warrior

Ancient Guardian

Darkness Series

Darkness Awakened

Taste of Darkness

Beyond the Darkness

Hunted by Darkness

Into the Darkness

Saved by Darkness

Guardian of Darkness

Sentinel of Darkness

A Very Dragon Christmas
Darkness Rising

Deadly Ops Series
Targeted
Bound to Danger
Chasing Danger
Shattered Duty
Edge of Danger
A Covert Affair

Endgame Trilogy
Bishop's Knight
Bishop's Queen
Bishop's Endgame

Holiday With a Hitman Series
How the Hitman Stole Christmas

MacArthur Family Series
Falling for Irish
Unintended Target
Saving Sienna

Moon Shifter Series
Alpha Instinct
Lover's Instinct
Primal Possession
Mating Instinct
His Untamed Desire
Avenger's Heat

Hunter Reborn

Protective Instinct

Dark Protector

A Mate for Christmas

O'Connor Family Series

Merry Christmas, Baby

Tease Me, Baby

It's Me Again, Baby

Mistletoe Me, Baby

Red Stone Security Series®

No One to Trust

Danger Next Door

Fatal Deception

Miami, Mistletoe & Murder

His to Protect

Breaking Her Rules

Protecting His Witness

Sinful Seduction

Under His Protection

Deadly Fallout

Sworn to Protect

Secret Obsession

Love Thy Enemy

Dangerous Protector

Lethal Game

Secret Enemy

Saving Danger

Guarding Her

Deadly Protector

Danger Rising

Protecting Rebel

Redemption Harbor® Series

Resurrection

Savage Rising

Dangerous Witness

Innocent Target

Hunting Danger

Covert Games

Chasing Vengeance

Redemption Harbor® Security

Fighting for Hailey

Fighting for Reese

Fighting for Adalyn

Sin City Series (the Serafina)

First Surrender

Sensual Surrender

Sweetest Surrender

Dangerous Surrender

Deadly Surrender

Verona Bay Series

Dark Memento

Deadly Past

Silent Protector

Linked books

Retribution

Tempting Danger

Non-series Romantic Suspense

Running From the Past

Dangerous Secrets

Killer Secrets

Deadly Obsession

Danger in Paradise

His Secret Past

Paranormal Romance

Destined Mate

Protector's Mate

A Jaguar's Kiss

Tempting the Jaguar

Enemy Mine

Heart of the Jaguar

Printed in the USA
CPSIA information can be obtained
at www.ICGtesting.com
LVHW050747290124
770207LV00004B/43